His Promises Had
Been Made to Be Broken.

'You shouldn't have done that!' Her colour deepened as she realised how ineffective and belated her protest was.

'Are you quite sure that's true? Can you honestly deny that you wanted me to kiss you?'

'We made a pact, Adam, and you've broken it.'

'Broken it? You're being absurd. We're husband and wife; surely a kiss is permissible? After all, we can live normally for the time you are here. Why not enjoy what is ours by right?'

ANNE HAMPSON
currently makes her home in Ireland, but this top romance author has travelled and lived all over the world. This variety of experience is reflected in her books, which present the ever-changing face of romance as it is found wherever people fall in love.

Dear Reader:

Silhouette Romances is an exciting new publishing venture. We will be presenting the very finest writers of contemporary romantic fiction as well as outstanding new talent in this field. It is our hope that our stories, our heroes and our heroines will give you, the reader, all you want from romantic fiction.

Also, *you* play an important part in our future plans for Silhouette Romances. We welcome any suggestions or comments on our books and I invite you to write to us at the address below.

So, enjoy this book and all the wonderful romances from Silhouette. They're for *you!*

Karen Solem
Editor-in-Chief
Silhouette Books
P.O. Box 769
New York, N.Y. 10019

ANNE HAMPSON
Man Without a Heart

Silhouette *Romance*

Published by Silhouette Books New York

America's Publisher of Contemporary Romance

Other Silhouette Romances by Anne Hampson

Payment in Full
Stormy Masquerade
The Dawn Steals Softly
Second Tomorrow
Man of the Outback
Where Eagles Nest

SILHOUETTE BOOKS, a Simon & Schuster Division of
GULF & WESTERN CORPORATION
1230 Avenue of the Americas, New York, N.Y. 10020

Distributed by Pocket Books

ISBN: 0-671-57052-8

First Silhouette printing January, 1981

10 9 8 7 6 5 4 3 2 1

America's Publisher of Contemporary Romance

Printed in the U.S.A.

Man Without a Heart

Chapter One

Why on earth her sister had become engaged to a Greek, Jill could not understand; still less did she understand why, less than a fortnight later, she should want to break it off. That wasn't all, though. Susie was asking Jill to go to Adamandios Doxaros and tell him of his fiancée's change of heart.

'Please do it for me,' Susie begged. 'It isn't asking much, is it?'

'Not asking much?' Jill blinked incredulously. 'I don't know how you can be so casual about it. I warned you that you were acting too hastily, not having known Adam for more than a month or so. I also warned you about Greek men in general. I've lived here in Athens, remember, and I've learnt enough about the Greek male to cause me to give him the widest berth possible.'

'I wish you wouldn't keep on reminding me of your warnings,' snapped Susie pettishly. 'If you hadn't invited me over here, I'd never have met the wretched man!'

Jill drew a deep breath. She had been working in Athens for over a year, ever since she and her sister had decided to live separate lives. It had been Susie's suggestion originally, and although the two girls got on together very well indeed, sharing the house left to them jointly by their parents, they had both expressed the opinion that it would be nice to have their complete independence. However, Jill felt that Susie at eighteen was rather young to be on her own, and she had wanted to wait another year at least. But Susie was insistent, resisting Jill's attitude, declaring that just because she was three years older she need not think she could rule her life.

Jill had been learning Greek as a hobby and decided to have a prolonged holiday in Greece in order to practise the language. The house which she and Susie had sold fetched more than either girl had anticipated, and so Jill found she could easily afford the holiday and still be able to buy a small house on her return. She had seen her sister settled first, in a flat she was sharing with another girl of her own age, and then she had set off for Greece. Within a month she heard of a vacancy at the travel agent's in Omonia Square, and because she could speak French as well as Greek, she was successful in obtaining the post. So instead of investing her money in a house in

England, she bought a little villa outside Athens, a white-and-blue villa with poinsettia hedges and bougainvillaeas climbing round the portals of the verandah. She had immediately invited Susie over, but Susie was already booked to go to Spain with her flatmate, Avril, so it was to be almost another year before she could come out to Greece. Jill had been thrilled when Susie wrote to say she would come, but did not quite understand the addition:

'I can stay for six weeks or longer, as I have given up my job and am not looking for another for a while.'

Jill had naturally been troubled but had decided not to write back for more information, knowing how strongly her sister resented any advice which Jill might at times offer.

With her own holidays due, Jill planned to take her sister around for the first fortnight, visiting Delphi and Olympia among other places of interest. After that Susie would have to be left to her own devices for the remainder of her holiday—at least, during the daytime while Jill was at work. Susie had somehow got to know and become friendly with an English couple living down the road from Jill, and it was they who took her to the party where she met the Greek millionaire Adam Doxaros. Susie had been most reticent right from the beginning, never even suggesting that Jill and Adam should meet. Nor had Adam taken his fiancée to meet his family. In fact, when Jill mentioned this, tentatively, in order not to arouse Susie's possible resentment, Susie had said that she did not even know if Adam had any relatives. This was eventually to prove to have been a lie on Susie's part.

'But surely he's told you something about himself?'

'Nothing,' Susie had replied, ignoring her sister's sceptical look.

'Don't you ever talk about yourselves?'

'Sometimes. I know he owns a cruise line and has a villa on an island somewhere.'

'I thought you said he lives in Athens?'

'He has a flat here— Oh, Jill, do you have to be so inquisitive about my affairs!'

'I'm worried, Susie. I know you dislike my taking on the role of elder sister, but you must admit I have reason for feeling perturbed about you. There's something definitely fishy about this whole business.'

Susie gave a deep sigh of asperity. 'He's a millionaire and he wants to marry me, so please let the matter drop!'

'Where is his home?' persisted Jill, determined not to be put off.

'I think the island's called Corina.'

'Corina. . . .' Jill became thoughtful. 'I can't think where it is, but I've read about it and it's very beautiful. A number of Greek shipping millionaires have settled there recently. It has wonderful beaches and a few archaeological sites.'

'Yes, Adam did mention those things.' Susie's voice was still sharp-edged, and Jill said no more, but as the days passed her sister became so morose that she just had to question her again.

'Are you quite happy about the engagement, Susie?'

A startled look, a long moment of silence, and then, defensively: 'Happy? Of course I'm happy! We're to be married in a week's time—'

'A *week!*' broke in Jill, her beautiful brown eyes wide with anxiety and bewilderment. 'Susie, you can't! What on earth's wrong with you? You don't know the man. Besides, you've not brought him here yet. I want to see him—and I want to question him about his family.'

'It has nothing at all to do with you, so you can just keep out of it!'

But Jill was no longer intending to be put off, and she continued to question Susie. There was no result, though, and eventually she had no alternative but to give up, telling herself that she had done all she could, under the circumstances. Susie was almost twenty now, and her own mistress.

It was only a day later that Susie, right out of the blue, asked Jill to see Adam and tell him the wedding was off, that Susie was not now willing to go through with it.

Relief flowed over Jill like a deluge, but alongside this was total bewilderment, because Susie would offer no explanation concerning her change of heart.

'I've never known you quite so close as this over anything,' complained Jill. 'It was puzzling enough when you became engaged to him; it's even more puzzling now that you've changed your mind.'

Susie frowned, then sighed—like a martyr, thought Jill with ever-growing impatience.

'If only you'd mind your own business,' snapped Susie. 'I'm not a child who needs minding all the time!'

Jill's colour rose. She had had just about enough of her sister's awkwardness and bad temper. 'All right, I will mind my own business! If you're intending to jilt this man, then do your own dirty work! There isn't any reason, anyway, why you should have asked me to see him. It's your place, and no one else's, to go and see him—'

'I can't! He's a hateful man! He's arrogant and domineering and . . . and . . . bossy! He'd strangle me!'

For fully thirty seconds Jill could only stare. Susie's eyes had filled up, and her hands were clenching and unclenching convulsively. Jill's astounded eyes moved to her sister's face, pale and lovely but drawn and strained. Her big blue eyes stared into space, her mouth trembled, as if she wanted to murmur something but found it impossible to articulate words.

'He's a hateful man . . . ?' Jill spoke at last, her whole manner one of bewilderment. 'Susie, nothing of this business makes sense to me.'

Susie looked at her, then burst into tears. 'I expect,' she managed after a while, 'th-that I'll have to . . . to tell y-you everything.'

'It would be an idea,' returned Jill, trying to keep the dry irony out of her voice.

Susie began to speak, and Jill learned that, while still in England, Susie had met and fallen in love with a young man, Kenneth Rivington, who owned a small grocer's shop not far from where she lived.

'We got engaged,' continued Susie, accepting the handkerchief offered by her sister, 'and I thought it would be easy to persuade him to give up the shop and take a proper job.' Susie paused to apply the handkerchief to her eyes.

'You never mentioned this engagement,' said Jill a trifle accusingly.

Susie shrugged her shoulders. 'It wasn't anyone's business but my own—and Ken's of course.'

'I suppose I can accept that.' Jill's voice had a curt edge despite the pity she felt for her sister. Susie was very young, really, very immature. 'This shop—why did you want him to give it up?'

'Because I couldn't see myself working behind a counter for the rest of my days!'

'I shouldn't think he'd expect you to. Is he managing on his own now?'

'He has one assistant. He says he'll have his own supermarket one day, and then he'll just do the supervising.'

'That sounds reasonable, and possible.'

'We quarrelled over it,' said Susie, ignoring Jill's comment. 'It was dreadful; he accused me of insincerity, said I didn't love him . . .' She spread her hands and the tears began to fall again. 'I do love him, Jill! And I want to marry him even if it does mean . . . mean w-working in that horrid shop all my life!'

'You gave up your own job. Why?'

'I wanted to get away from him—from the flat and Avril and everyone! I thought I'd come here to you for a time and try to forget Ken, but I couldn't!'

Jill fell thoughtfully silent for a while, her mind quickly sorting out the whole situation—at least, as far as Susie was concerned. The attitude of the Greek was one that still baffled Jill exceedingly.

'You became engaged to Adam on the rebound—or even for spite.' A statement to which Susie nodded her head in agreement.

'It was mainly for spite. I had the idea of writing to Ken and telling him I was marrying a millionaire.'

'And you find you can't.'

'No, I can never marry anyone but Ken.'

Jill was very tempted to censure her sister but thought better of it. She was far too unhappy already, and scared, too, of the Greek.

'What makes you so afraid of this man Adam?' she asked curiously.

'He . . . he threatened me—well, not exactly threatened, but advised, in that quiet voice with its foreign accent . . . Oh, Jill, he has a way of speaking that frightens you! He's like a devil, a pagan—the Greeks were all pagans once, you know.'

'And so was every other nation," was Jill's dry response. 'I can't see why you're so scared of the man, just because he has a certain way of speaking. What about this advice he gave you?'

'He said—because I think he knew that I

wanted to change my mind almost from the first—that I'd better keep to my promise, because if I didn't, I'd live to regret it.'

'Not very loverlike, I must say!' Jill knew of course that Greek men rarely fell in love. They married for the physical enjoyment and convenience of having a wife. They assumed the role of master, often tyrannical in their dealings with the women of the family. Wives were totally subjected to the wills of their husbands.

'I knew he wasn't marrying me for love.'

'You knew?' Jill frowned. 'Then why in heaven's name did you become engaged to him?'

Susie hesitated a moment and then resignedly confessed, 'He made a bargain with me. He has an aged mother who's fretting because none of her three sons is married. Also, Adam's always been something of a rake—'

'He told you this!' exclaimed Jill disbelievingly.

Susie shook her head. Her golden hair caught the sunlight streaming through the large window of the sitting room, and Jill, looking at her with a critical eye, thought she had never seen a girl as beautiful as her sister. But Susie's beauty, although Jill didn't see it, had a pale, ethereal quality that gave the impression of weakness, of lack of character. Jill, on the other hand, was possessed of stronger features, classical features which had been likened by a Greek friend of hers to those of the goddess Athena herself. Her forehead was high, unlined above delicately arched brows. Her eyes were large and deeply brown, with a frankness and sincerity which made people trust her immediately. Her mouth was wide and generous, her chin pointed and strong. Her hair was a glory of russet brown, gleaming and curly, with a delightful little fringe which flicked to one side of her forehead in several half-curls that were often unruly, making her look younger than her twenty-three years.

'No, he didn't tell me,' Susie was saying, as she applied the handkerchief to her eyes again. 'I reached that conclusion myself from things he said now and then. He has what they call pillow friends here; they're really—'

'Yes, Greek men usually do have pillow friends,' broke in Jill casually. 'But they usually give them up when they marry—at least, for a while. They might then go back to them, I don't really know. All I do know is that they're an amorous lot and seem to think of little else but sex.'

'I got the same impression, although Adam has never tried to make love to me.' Susie paused a moment. 'I was telling you about our bargain. He wants to set his mother's mind at rest—I got the impression he worships her, despite the sort of a man he is otherwise.'

'The Greeks revere their parents. You never find an aged person entering an institution, not here in Greece.'

'Well, Adam decided to make his mother happy and so he looked round for a wife. I met him and he seemed very interested in me. I was flattered, but later he was very honest and told me why he wanted to marry me. He'd give me everything in the way of luxury, and a very big settlement when, after his mother's death, we had a divorce.'

Jill shook her head, even now unable to take in the whole incredible situation. For her sister to consent to such a bargain was completely beyond her comprehension.

'And you really believed you could do it?'

Susie heaved a sigh and said no, she had never really believed she could do it.

'But I felt I would force myself,' she added inconsistently. 'You see, I thought it would be worth it—all that money coming to me in a very short time, as his mother's in her seventies and has a weak heart. And it wasn't as if Adam was going to force his attentions on me. . . .' Susie's voice faded out as she saw the sceptical expression that spread over her sister's face. 'I believe he'd have kept to his side of the bargain,' she added defensively at last.

'Then you're far more naïve than I thought,' returned Jill dryly. 'No Greek, my dear, could have a woman in his house and leave her alone for long. I've just told you, they think of little else but sex.'

'I'm sure you're exaggerating. In any case, he'd not bother me with his attentions when he has other women who'd be willing—as I'm sure I wouldn't be!'

Jill could have laughed outright, but she resisted doing so, the occasion not being in any way right for the introduction of humour. 'Will-ing or not,' she said, 'you'd have been made to perform your wifely duties.'

Susie frowned. 'Don't be so crude, Jill!'

'All right, I won't. Now, about this business of telling him you're not going through with the marriage. You'll have to tell him yourself, Susie. It's not right to shirk it, and no matter what your fears, he can't hurt you.'

'You've forgotten already that he's said I'll live to regret it if I don't keep my promise. You see, I have a feeling—no, I'm absolutely sure—that he's told his mother about our engagement, because he mentioned the other day that she's much happier and has rallied from her melan-cholia, which was greatly troubling Adam, be-cause she'd said she was going to die a very unhappy woman.'

Jill gave a deep, impatient sigh. 'Threats or no, you'll have to face the man. I can't do it, Susie. Not that I wouldn't, don't think that. But in my opinion you owe it to this Adam to face him courageously and make your confession.'

Even as Jill was speaking, her sister was flicking a hand impatiently.

'I haven't any courage—you know full well I haven't! You've been the strong one, always. Look how you coped when Mummy and Daddy were killed in that accident. You cried and cried, as I did, but you coped, and we managed to keep the house on only your salary until I left school and could contribute. I remember so well your saying that at all costs we must keep the house—and you were only seventeen and a half then.'

Jill's thoughts strayed momentarily to that dreadful time when, from being a happy family, they were suddenly left on their own, just two girls, one only fourteen and a half. . . .

It had been a struggle, with Jill throwing up her chances of reaching university and immediately getting herself a job. She had been lucky in her employer, who after listening to her story gave her a starting salary of more than she would have received anywhere else. He had died later, but left her a small legacy which enabled her to meet some of the debts that had inevitably piled up.

Susie was speaking again, breaking into her reverie, and Jill brought her attention to the present, and the matter of informing the Greek that Susie was not now willing to marry him.

'Do it for me, Jill. I can't face him—I *can't!*'

'I'm sure he's not as bad as you make out, Susie.'

'He looked like a fiend when he was telling me I'd regret it if I changed my mind.'

'Well, he might *look* like a fiend, but he daren't injure you. Make up your mind, Susie, and do the right thing.'

'You're refusing? That's your last word?'

'I won't let you shirk what's your duty,' said Jill firmly, and as she was suddenly diverted by the ancient Greek gardener whom she shared with two others in the area, she failed to notice the expression that came to her sister's face.

But the following day, when Jill returned from work, it was to find a note on the table informing her that Susie had gone home, having been fortunate enough to book a seat on a plane leaving the Athens airport at one-thirty that day.

The car standing outside her garden gate did not even attract Jill's attention; the road was very quiet and dark and it was usual for cars to be parked along it while their owners walked to the *taverna* a few hundred yards away on the main street. She had been out to a meal at the home of a Greek friend, a young woman who worked in the bank which was next door to the travel agency where Jill was employed, and so it was much later than usual when she arrived home. It was as she fumbled in the dark with the little gate, whose latch was difficult to undo, that her senses suddenly became alert, not immediately to danger, but rather to the fact that two men had been sitting in the car, in the dark, for as she stood there they got out and came toward her. It was as they drew close that fear entered into her and she felt the presence of danger. Her hands began to tremble, but to her relief she managed to unlatch the gate. That was all; she was unable to take even one step along the path. A hand was thrust around her and pressed over her mouth; she was lifted bodily, struggling but unable to scream for help, and within seconds she was in the car and a blindfold fastened over her eyes. She heard the two men talking in Greek, something about being taken on a boat of some sort. The car shot forward, the jerk sending her head hard against the window. Bright lights spun behind her eyes and, more from fear than pain, she drifted into unconsciousness.

She opened her eyes and all was dark except for a strange disk of muted light which seemed a very long way off. Dreaming. . . . Yes, she'd had the most horrible nightmare, where she was kidnapped by two men—

It was no dream! She sat up, fear sweeping over her like a deluge as memory returned, and noticed that she had been lying on a bunk. Where was she? Where were the two men who had carried her off? She turned and slid off the bed. Her legs were like jelly, but she moved carefully toward the disk of muted purple light. A porthole. The moment this registered, she became aware of the throbbing of engines and remembered that she had heard the men saying something about a boat. Where were they taking her? How long would she be on this vessel? What time was it? Was there a light switch? She began moving around, amazed that her mind could be so clear when fear was holding her so mercilessly in its grip. She was searching for an electric switch and knew that she would very likely find one. It came to her hand at last and she blinked for a moment or two as the cabin was flooded with light. It was a luxurious cabin, with highly polished woodwork and furniture. A wardrobe was on one wall and a dressing table on another. The bed she had been lying on occupied the wall opposite the door, which was on the same side of

the cabin as the wardrobe. Jill saw her light-
weight coat on a chair, her handbag on top of it.
She glanced at her watch and saw that it was
half-past two. The throbbing of the engines
seemed to become louder and louder until it
became a drumming in her ears. She tried the
door, then began thumping on the panels with
her fists. No sound except that deafening drumming of the engines! She would go mad! Her
glance went round the cabin again and lit on a
metal wastebasket. Picking it up, she banged on
the door, marking the beautiful wood and even
splintering it in places.

At last she heard voices, then, after what
seemed an eternity, the sound of shuffling footsteps and the repeated murmur of voices.

'Be quiet! What do you want?' The words came
in strongly accented English.

What did she want? Was the man soft in the
head to ask a question like that?

'I want to get out of here! Open this door—'

'Thank heaven she's awakened!' The voice
was that of a second man, speaking in Greek.
'She's been unconscious a long time.'

Jill wondered whether to hammer on the door
again, just to see what would happen, but she
thought better of it, deciding to listen instead to
the two men talking. Her Greek was not so good
that she caught every single word, but it was
certainly good enough for her to understand all
that was being said.

'I'll be glad when we're there and can hand
her over to the master.'

'It won't be long now.'

'She was so afraid, Petros, and I couldn't help thinking that if it was my daughter, my little Maria—'

'Your daughter would not be carried off like this one, Georgios. Why should she be? So what's the use of talking about it?'

'This English girl,' said Georgios, bypassing Petros' words, 'was so frightened. You should have made it clear to her that she would come to no real harm.'

'She didn't give me the chance! She fainted before I could tell her anything.' The voice faded and Jill realised that the men were walking away. She cried out, crashing the wastebasket against the door again.

'Go to sleep, woman,' shouted Petros. 'It will be light in an hour and I'll bring you some breakfast!' She decided not to court trouble by making a bigger fuss and getting him even more angry than he sounded already. She had been calmed by Georgios' words: 'You should have made it clear to her that she would come to no real harm.'

Besides the calm, though, there was puzzlement. If no harm were meant her, then why had she been abducted at all?

She sat down, trying to think, but realising that she was very, very tired. It would be easiest to get back on that bed and try to sleep for an hour. At least she was safe for the present, and it seemed very much as if she would continue to be safe.

Many questions darted about in her mind as she lay on the bed a moment or two later, questions about her kidnapping, about this 'master' to whom she was being taken, but gradually the questions ran into one another as her mind became more and more hazy with the approach of the soothing slumber that she craved.

Daylight was streaming through the porthole when, awakened by the door opening, Jill sat up on the bed and quickly slid off it.

Petros had brought a tray, which he deposited on a small table at the foot of the bunk bed. 'We'll be there in half an hour,' he told her. 'You will be taken to my master.'

'Who is your master?'

The man shrugged and turned to the door. 'My master say that we must not speak to the lady,' and with that he was gone. Jill watched the door frowningly, heard the key turn in the lock, and then, with a little sigh that was a mingling of resignation and bewilderment, she determinedly sat down to tackle the contents of the tray. She might as well face this 'master' on a full stomach rather than an empty one, she thought, eyeing the crispy rolls, the fresh butter and the cherry jam. The coffeepot was hot to her touch, and the cream in the jug was thick and fresh.

The engines stopped a short while later and she looked out the porthole to see a charming little harbour surrounded, except for the narrow strait through which the boat had come, by pine woods, olive and palm trees, and orange groves. The land to the east looked steep, with a pyramid of blue and white houses gleaming in the sunshine. Next to the harbour itself, men sat mending nets or just chatting to one another. One man was slapping an octopus on the hard surface, creating a lather which, Jill had already learned, made the flesh tender and juicy. A donkey was ambling up a hillside, its back laden with brushwood; its owner rode another donkey, while his wife trudged along beside the laden donkey, a stick in her hand. Familiar sights. Jill had visited several Greek islands while she had been living in the capital, and she naturally wondered which one this was. Not one that she had visited, but its distance from Athens could not be very great.

It was only six o'clock when Petros entered the cabin again, this time to tell her that she was to be taken by car to his master.

She merely nodded, having already decided that to argue or question would be to no avail. Better wait until she came face to face with the man's employer, for only then would all the baffling questions be answered.

'Are you ready?' asked Petros.

'Yes, quite ready.' She picked up her coat and handbag. Her face was pale, but because of Georgios' reassuring words, she had completely lost that terrible fear which had sent every nerve in her body rioting and her heart throbbing wildly.

Chapter Two

The house appeared after the car had turned off
a narrow tree-shaded lane and into the drive
which, overhung with trees and flaunting exotic
flowering bushes for the whole of its winding
length, had caused the villa to be hidden from
view until they were almost upon it. Georgios
was driving the huge white car, Petros sitting in
the back with Jill, alertly watching her all the
time.

'We're there at last,' grunted Petros in his
accented English. 'And I am not sorry.'

'Nor am I,' said Jill, but to herself. Her eyes
were taking in the beautiful white villa with its
bright blue shutters and gaily coloured sun-
blinds. A verandah running the length of the
front façade seemed to be dripping with exotic

flowers; the arched front door, approached by a flight of white marble steps, had stone portals smothered in magenta bougainvillaea; in a shady courtyard seen through an archway of rambler roses, a fountain played, its waters stealing all the colours of the rainbow from the sun. The villa's setting was the most picturesque Jill had ever seen; it was set on a plateau on the hillside with a view of the bay and the strait on one side and of a pine forest on the other. White-sailed luxury yachts could be seen anchored in the bay, and there seemed to be flowers everywhere, growing in the hedgerows or flourishing in the gardens of the pretty villas scattered about the hillsides or along the flatter region down by the bay.

The whole atmosphere was warm and friendly, and as Jill slid from the car, she could scarcely imagine the owner of such a property being mixed up in anything as criminal as a kidnapping.

Petros escorted her to the door, his hand clutching her arm. He need not have been so cautious; Jill had no intention of making a run for it. She knew that she would not get very far before someone caught her, for now that she was out of the car, she saw no fewer than three gardeners at work in various parts of the grounds.

The door was opened by a Greek smartly dressed in a pair of black trousers, a white shirt and a grey linen jacket.

'The woman!' said Petros, giving Jill a push which sent her past the manservant and into the hall. 'Mind she doesn't escape.' The last sentence was spoken in Greek, and the man nodded his head. He closed the door and turned to Jill.

'This way, miss,' he said briefly, and Jill found herself following him toward a door at the far end of the hall. The servant opened the door after knocking and waiting for the invitation to enter.

'The lady, Mr. Adam,' he said, and Jill gave a sudden start on hearing that name. The servant seemed to disappear into air, so quickly did he make his departure. Jill, standing just inside the room, with the door closed behind her, could scarcely think clearly with the name 'Adam' repeating itself in her brain, and in addition, the attitude of the man who, sitting at a massive oak desk, had not yet even looked up from the paper he was perusing, seemed somehow quietly disturbing.

Jill coughed, and he said quietly, but with a harsh edge to his faintly accented voice, 'So, my little runaway, you'd go back on your word, eh—' He had glanced up as he spoke, breaking off abruptly when his very dark brown eyes encountered Jill's slender form on the other side of the desk. 'Good heavens! Who the devil are you?' His expression was one of scowling disbelief. 'What the devil—?' He stopped again and stared, rising from his chair. 'How did you get here?' he demanded so belligerently that Jill's hackles were instantly up. Her brown eyes glinted and her mouth went tight. That he was completely staggered by the sight of her was plain, which was not surprising, the truth having been made plain by his first words. It was her sister who was to have been abducted. For a fleeting space Jill stared at him with as belligerent an expression as any he himself could produce. She was noticing the flexed jawline and firm, dominant chin, the sensuous mouth that carried the ruthless lines she had seen in the stone statues in the museums of Athens, statues of his pagan ancestors. His nose was straight, his cheekbones high, his skin a rich deep bronze, unlined and clear. Her eyes moved to his forehead, and to the widow's peak wedging deeply into it.

She spoke while continuing her examination of him, her attention on his body now—a tall, lithe body with wide, powerful shoulders and narrow hips. 'Your second question is superfluous, Mr. Doxaros, since it was on your orders that I was attacked by two ruffians and bundled into a car, then onto a boat and then into another car, which brought me here. The answer to your first question is that I am Susie's sister, Jill Harris.'

His eyes opened wide. 'They took the wrong girl. . . . The damned idiots! I'll flay them alive!' He looked so savage that for a moment Jill really believed he would carry out his threat. 'Idiots!' he repeated. 'I told them that the girl had blond hair and blue eyes!'

'It was dark when they abducted me,' returned Jill tartly. 'You can't blame them for the blunder; it was poor organisation,' she added finally, because she just had to get at him.

His eyes glinted, but any retort that came to his lips was stemmed, and it was plain to Jill that he was not going to waste time on irrelevancies. He had suddenly become interested in her, examining her thoughtfully, his eyes first on her hair, short and curling and the colour of beech leaves in autumn, then on her face with its clear alabaster skin through which the blue veins on her temples could clearly be seen, her mouth, her eyes, big and honest and framed by curling dark lashes. In the cabin there had been a shower alcove and Jill had been able to make use of it. In her handbag she had a blusher and lip rouge, and despite her situation, she had spent a little time on her appearance, firm in the belief that, with a woman, her degree of confidence was increased if she knew she was looking her best.

'Where is your sister?' demanded the Greek at last.

'In England—out of your way!'

He nodded frowningly. 'She phoned me to say she was breaking the engagement. I said she couldn't do it, but she rang off immediately. I called at the house; she was out, but I felt it would be simple to catch her sometime, and I set my men to watch the house. . . .' He tailed off, his ruthless mouth compressing. 'How in the devil's name they managed to take the wrong girl, I don't know. I warned them that there was a sister. I'll deal with that later, though. For the present—well, I owe you an apology.' He was suddenly the gentleman, gracious and smiling. 'Please sit down, Miss Harris, and let us talk.

You must have learned something from Susie as to the reason for our engagement?'

Jill found herself moving to the chair he had brought forward for her. One part of her mind was concerned with getting out of here, getting back home, to telephone her employer and give him some sort of excuse for her absence from work. The other half of her mind, though, was intrigued by the whole situation. She would have been less than human if she had not been exceedingly curious to learn a little more about it.

'Will you have some refreshments, Miss Harris?' Adam Doxaros spoke as she sat down, pulling a bell rope without waiting for her answer. He talked while waiting for his manservant; Jill listened intently, and all the while she was taking in his appearance, deciding that in spite of the extreme severity of his features he was without doubt the most handsome and distinguished man she had ever met. He was cultured and highly intelligent, and it soon struck Jill that he would have become bored in no time at all by a green girl like her sister.

By the time the manservant arrived, he had already given Jill a clear picture of what he had in mind when he asked Susie to marry him.

'It was purely a business deal,' he was saying when the servant knocked and entered. 'Coffee?' he inquired of Jill. 'Or a cool drink? Lemonade? We grow our own lemons here.'

'I'll have coffee, please.'

'Coffee it is.' And then, as the thought suddenly occurred to him: 'Do you want something to

eat? Did you manage to eat anything for breakfast?'

His meaning was quite clear, and to her
amazement Jill found herself smiling in amusement.

'You're wondering if I was so paralysed by fear
that I couldn't eat? No, Mr. Doxaros, I wasn't
paralysed by fear. I thoroughly enjoyed the
breakfast you so thoughtfully provided.' The last
sentence was spoken with a distinctly acid
touch; Adam smiled now, as if he too were
seeing something faintly amusing in the fact
that she had been able to tuck into the breakfast
that had been given her. His servant went off,
and Adam, as she was already thinking of him,
resumed his narrative, putting his listener in
possession of several important facts that Susie
had omitted to mention. However, in the main,
he was only repeating what Susie had already
said.

'You seem very, very concerned about your
mother.' Jill spoke after a short silence during
which she had been going over some of the
information imparted to her. She was deeply
impressed by the Greek's anxiety over his mother's health, and by his sincere love for her. She
had known, of course, that in Greece, more than
in any other country in the world, old people
were tenderly cared for by their relatives. They
were looked up to, and although the Greek
woman was servile in her youth and middle age,
she became the queen of her household once she
grew old.

'It's a natural thing, Miss Harris. You say you have lived in my country for over a year, so you must have learned of our concern for the elderly people of our families.'

She nodded her head. 'Yes, I have.'

'My mother will die happy only if I am married. Greek women are like that; they want to see their sons married. My father died an unhappy man, I'm sorry to say, because I was unwilling to marry just to please him. As I have mentioned, I'm secretly engaged to the daughter of a business acquaintance, and we shall marry when my mother dies. But Mother hates this girl, being convinced that she would never make me happy. The idea that I would marry her would be appalling to my mother, hence my insistence on a secret engagement.'

'This young lady doesn't mind if you marry someone else in the meantime?' Jill was frowning, wondering what kind of a girl would be willing for her fiancé to enter into a temporary marriage with someone else.

'She has no option,' returned Adam inflexibly. 'It is I who am in control of the situation.' His mouth had set, his eyes become hard. 'In Greece the female does as she is bid—but you must have learned that also.'

The servant had entered with the tray, which he put down on the corner of Adam's desk. 'Will there be anything else, Mr. Adam?' he asked respectfully.

'Not at the moment, Andonys, but I think we might be having a guest for lunch—'

'Oh, no,' broke in Jill hurriedly. 'I want to leave on the first boat—' She stopped suddenly. 'I don't even know where I am!' she exclaimed.

'You're on the island of Corina. You'll have an idea of its location when I tell you its southern shores run parallel to the shores of the Argolid.'

She nodded but made no comment. The man-servant went out, closing the door quietly behind him, and Adam busied himself with the coffee. He handed her a cup, and held out the sugar for her to help herself.

'It's a pity that Susie became scared and ran off like that,' he said frowningly. 'But I found her extremely young and immature. Flighty, too—and obviously unreliable.'

Jill ignored that. 'I really must be leaving, Mr. Doxaros. What time is the ferry?'

He made no answer; she watched with frowning perplexity as he moved away from her and stood by the window. The sunlight streamed past him, filtered by the leaves of a jacaranda tree which was in full bloom, its beautiful blue flowers appearing to be a delicate veil moving gently in the breeze. Shadows were cast onto the dark face, and although this seemed to accentuate the severity of the man's features, Jill still found them inordinately handsome. There was something about him that attracted her in a strange unfathomable way which was as disturbing as it was exciting. Yes, she was ready to admit to herself that the man excited her—by his personality, by his looks, by his superiority and the dominance of his manner. She found to her amazement that she had already forgiven him for the action that had, initially, put such terror into her.

At last he turned and looked directly at her. 'Will you take your sister's place, Miss Harris?'

'Me!' She stared at him incredulously. 'Are you serious?'

'As I have said, I need someone—anyone—to marry. I have never taken Susie to see Mother, but I have told my mother that I've met an English girl whom I am seriously thinking of asking to marry me. So naturally Mother's become excited by the prospect of having a daughter-in-law at last.' He shook his head and glanced again at Jill. 'I can't now tell her that it is all off—I won't tell her!'

Jill spread her hands. 'You'll have to, Mr. Doxaros, since I'm not going to take Susie's place. No, I wouldn't even consider such a stupid act! You must think me a lunatic!'

'You haven't even given the matter a thought, Miss Harris.'

'And I don't intend to!'

'The reward would be very great. I promised Susie a large settlement—'

'Well, you can keep your settlement,' interrupted Jill. 'It so happens that I'm not all that interested in money!'

'My mother . . . will you not consent to a meeting with her? She's a dear and gracious lady who is sad and brooding because none of her sons is married. You would like my mother, Miss Harris.'

'I won't argue the point, but her well-being has nothing to do with me. Why, the whole idea of marrying you is so preposterous that I'm not willing to continue discussing it!' Jill drained her coffeecup and replaced it on the saucer with a little bang. She was trembling, her heart fluttering in the strangest way, and her mind sending out warning lights, advising her to make as hasty a departure from here as possible.

'It would be a temporary marriage,' Adam told her perseveringly. 'I'd ask nothing from you, naturally. I have my friends—'

'And that's another thing,' she interrupted, vaguely aware that she was on the defensive, which was stupid, since there was not the remotest possibility of Adam's being able to persuade her to marry him. 'You openly admit to having pillow friends—'

'Where did you hear that expression,' he demanded, as if hearing it from her lips angered him.

'Does it matter?' she returned heatedly. 'You admit to having these women, and to having a fiancée too. Doesn't she mind that you're unfaithful to her?' asked Jill, for the moment diverted.

'My dear Miss Harris,' said Adam in some amusement, 'all Greek men are unfaithful. No, she doesn't mind at all. It's purely a business arrangement, her father and I wishing to combine the two shipping lines, his and mine. There never was any question of love between Julia and me. She'll have her lovers eventually, when we are married, so why should she object to my having mine?'

Jill shook her head bewilderdly. 'It's incredible! Is a Greek never jealous? Does he never resent his wife receiving the attentions of other men?'

He laughed, appearing to be greatly amused by her indignation. 'There has to be love for there to be jealousy, Miss Harris, and Greek men never fall in love.'

'I don't believe that they *never* fall in love!'

'Very well,' he conceded, 'they rarely fall in love.'

'Couldn't you ever be jealous, Mr. Doxaros?' She could not have explained why she put the question, but she was profoundly interested in his reply to it.

His eyes glinted suddenly and he looked so fiendish that an involuntary shiver passed along Jill's spine.

'If, by the remotest possibility, I should find myself in love with a woman, then, yes, I'd be jealous—so much so that I'd make her pay beyond her wildest dreams if she allowed another man to pay her more than the superficial requirements of courtesy and respect.'

Jill drew a breath, her mind bringing unwanted visions of Adam, her husband, turning dark, angry eyes toward her as he slowly crossed the room.

Good heavens, where were her thoughts taking her?

'The ferry,' she began, looking at her watch. 'I expect there is one?'

'You won't see my mother?'

'No, definitely not! The suggestion that I marry you is ridiculous—I've already told you so!'

'It's your last word?' He mentioned a sum of money which he was prepared to give her when they were divorced. 'You won't consider it, and the advantage to yourself?'

She shook her head vigorously. 'It's my last word, Mr. Doxaros! I wouldn't dream of marrying you!'

Jill sat in the garden, reading a book. The sun was becoming too hot, but her tan was progressing so beautifully that she was determined to remain out on the lawn a little while longer. She put the book down on the grass and allowed her mind to wander. Even now, a month later, she was staggered by her action in marrying Adam. There had been no sign of wavering until she met Mrs. Doxaros. Adam had brought the old lady to Jill's villa, and from the moment of meeting her, Jill had felt herself to be trapped.

It had been a clever move on Adam's part, because when he introduced his mother to her he had sent a pleading look in Jill's direction, asking her not to say anything that would upset the older woman. Jill knew she would remember that meeting for the rest of her life. Mrs. Doxaros had been less frail than Jill expected, but that she was in poor health was apparent from the difficulty she had with her breathing. From the first moment the old lady had acted as though Jill were to be her daughter-in-law and, being so softhearted, Jill had found it quite

impossible to disillusion her. There was no need
at the moment, Jill told herself, but later she
would give Adam Doxaros a piece of her mind
and tell him to get out of the mess as best he
could. But after a while Jill found herself drawn
irresistibly to the old lady, and the attraction
was obviously mutual. Adam had come to Jill's
home later, and although she had fought
against his persuasions at first, the sweet, lined
face of his mother persistently intruded and in
the end Jill owned to being utterly defeated.

And after that she was able to review the
situation without the strong emotions that had
been with her at first. The marriage—as Adam
had from the first asserted—was going to benefit
everyone concerned. Mrs. Doxaros was going to
be happy, so happy that Jill could not but feel
happy herself at having the chance of bringing
contentment to a lady she had been so strongly
attracted to almost immediately. Second, Jill
herself was to benefit, financially, beyond her
wildest dreams. The sum Adam had promised
would make her rich, and meanwhile, she
would enjoy the luxury of his home on Corina,
and perhaps his flat in Athens, and she would
have a monthly allowance far in excess of her
needs. She could have her own friends—male
and female—so long as none of her actions
interfered with his mother's happiness. All
these Adam had promised.

Yes, decided Jill, it *was* all good, this arrangement. There were no complications that she
could see, no probable circumstances that
would bring friction between her husband and

herself. He was to go his way and she hers. He would take his fiancée out when he was in Athens, or for a trip on his yacht now and then—leaving his wife at home, of course. He would have his pillow friends, his other friends. Jill did not rule out the possibility of meeting a young man—there were lots of Englishmen working in Athens—and falling in love. She would have to explain the position to him, and ask him to wait until she gained her freedom. Meanwhile, they could be friends and go about together. Adam would not mind—in fact, he would probably be glad that she had found someone, some very special friend whom she would marry later, when she and her husband were divorced.

And so it was with a happy mind, totally free from qualms, that Jill had agreed to marry Adam. They had the ceremony in Athens, Adam bringing his mother over in the yacht from Corina. She lived in a small villa two miles from Adam's house, and was looked after by two servants, Sophia and her husband, Drakos, both of whom adored her. The wedding breakfast was attended by several of Adam's friends, one or two of whom teased Jill, asking her how she managed to breach his defences and end his bachelorhood. She had smiled and managed very well to keep up a pretence. Adam had congratulated her, and the short voyage back from Piraeus to Corina had been a most pleasant one for Jill. She got her bearings around the yacht, enjoyed her mother-in-law's company, got along fine with her husband. And now, after a month of marriage, she still had no regrets. Life was good, and smooth—no complications, nothing to disrupt in any way the harmony of her life with Adam.

He came from the villa, his tall frame clad in a pair of dark blue shorts and a short-sleeved white shirt. She could not help staring at him—as she did so often lately—and admiring his looks and bearing, his masculinity. He saw her, and she smiled, expecting a smile in response, but she was subjected to a frown instead.

'You're going to suffer for this,' he said sternly. 'The sun should be taken in small doses. You lie in it for too long all at once.'

She shrugged, but reached for her wrap. It was a pretty coral-coloured little coat fashioned and made in Paris. Adam had brought it back from one of his visits to Athens. She had been amused, remembering his admission about pillow friends, and wondered if he had happened to buy two of these at the same time.

He glanced casually at her as she put it on, then remarked on the colour, saying he must remember that coral suited her complexion.

'I ought to take you to Athens to do some shopping,' he added thoughtfully. 'You haven't a very extensive wardrobe, I've noticed.'

'I don't really need one,' she pointed out. 'I don't go anywhere much.'

He sat down on the grass, idly picking up her book to glance at the title. 'I hope, Jill, that you won't become discontented. I'm fully aware that it must be dull for you—'

'I'm very happy, Adam,' she interrupted, anxious to reassure him. 'In any case, I've made a bargain with you, and I'd never let you down.' The sincerity of her voice held his attention as she continued, her beautiful brown eyes looking into his, 'I know what my obligations are regarding your mother. It isn't possible that I would ever give her cause for suspecting that all was not well between you and me.'

She was relieved to see his face clear. He smiled, and she felt her heart flutter in the strangest way. The sensation was by no means new, but as yet she had not been strongly enough affected by it to ask herself for a reason. Her husband was so handsome that he was bound to affect her in some small way; this she had accepted from the start, and she did wonder how his fiancée had not fallen in love with him.

'Have you seen Mother today?' Adam asked a few moments later.

'No, I'm going along this afternoon—around four—to take tea with her.'

'She's very fond of you,' he said.

'And I of her. She's a marvellous person, Adam. She's like a goddess.'

He looked at her in some amusement. 'My wife is a romantic, eh? Been reading Greek mythology?'

She laughed, drawing her coat around her because she was quite suddenly conscious of her husband's eyes roving over her near-naked figure. 'I've always been interested in Greek mythology, and the country and people.'

'And so you decided to learn the language.'

'Yes, it was so difficult at first, though, that I almost gave up. However, I convinced myself that with perseverance I'd master it in the end, and I have.' She stopped, and this time her laugh was one of self-deprecation. 'I'm not terribly good at it, though,' she added finally.

'You're very good at it, Jill. I find it amazing that you've become so fluent.'

'Well, I have been in Greece for over a year, remember.'

He nodded, fell quiet for a space and then, right out of the blue: 'Have you heard from Susie lately?'

'About a fortnight ago,' answered Jill, thinking of her sister's reaction on learning of Jill's marriage to Adam. Susie had been furious, saying she, Jill, ought not to have pandered to Adam's whim. It was grasping and mercenary of Jill to make a bargain like that with Adam.

'Why should you get all that money?' Susie had written, having made a wild guess at the amount Jill would receive when eventually the marriage was dissolved. 'I hope, Jill, that you'll accept that it was through me that you met and married Adam, and will give me my share of the profits.' Jill had ignored that, and when she wrote—waiting awhile to allow her anger to abate—she had merely made her letter a short, chatty one containing scarcely any information about her life on the island of Corina. Susie seemed to have become discontented once again with Kenneth, and Jill was left guessing as to whether or not the couple were still keeping company.

'Is she going to marry that young man of hers?'

'I don't know. She doesn't seem to be very happy at the moment.' Jill had told Adam about Kenneth, feeling that she had to make some excuse for her sister's hasty action in running out on Adam.

'She's a strange girl,' mused Adam, opening the book he held and flicking through the pages. 'I really felt she was greedy enough to go through with our marriage. It was a surprise to me when she hinted one day that she was not sure whether she had made the right decision or not.'

'So you threatened her—well, she called it advice. You said that if she changed her mind she would regret it.'

'I did, but I knew of course that I couldn't really force her to keep her promise. I felt that if I abducted her and had her here, a prisoner, I could coerce her into keeping to the contract we had made.'

Jill looked at him, at the stern inflexibility of his features. There was certainly something pagan about him in this moment. He looked ruthless, wicked, a man without a heart.

'You think she would have responded to your . . . er . . . coercion?' asked Jill interestedly.

'She might have. I had the idea of making the reward such that she couldn't possibly resist it—that was, of course, if all else failed.'

'All else?' Jill's voice still held its note of interest. 'Just what does that mean, Adam?'

For a few seconds he hesitated, as if debating on the best way to frame his words. 'Well, to be quite honest, Jill, I did have in mind that I'd threaten to "take her" if she didn't agree to the marriage.'

Jill found herself colouring, yet she was able to say, 'And if you had threatened, and she had still remained adamant—for she *was* in love with someone else, remember—would you have carried out your threat?'

He smiled faintly and said, with the sort of inflexibility which brooked no argument, 'As the situation never arose, Jill, we shall not discuss it further.'

Again she coloured. This was not the first time her husband had admonished her in this subtle but very effective way he had. She wondered what it would be like to be really married to him. He would be the undisputed master, that was for sure. His wife would learn to obey him—or take the consequences.

That evening they went out to dine at the hotel on the edge of the bay. The lights of the yachts and fishing boats seemed to add romance to the moonlit sea and argent hillsides, the palms waving against a nebulous background of deep purple; the *bouzouki* music played while the dinner was being served on a wide verandah where coloured lamps, hidden in the trellis of vines, provided the only illumination for the tables. Jill was dressed in mauve, in an evening gown which, cut on the princess line, revealed with subtle allure the beautiful curves of her body. Between courses they danced; she felt the strength of her husband's frame pressed to hers. The experience was not new; every Greek man danced like that—holding the woman as if she were his personal property—but this time Jill was vitally affected by Adam's nearness, by the tingling warmth of his hand on her bare back, of his face above hers as his chin touched her hair. He seemed masterful, possessive, overpoweringly dominant. She was flushed when he brought her back to their table, and she could not help noticing the odd expression that came to his eyes. Was it desire? she wondered fearfully. She had put her whole trust in his word, and she had to admit that it was a little late now to remind herself of her warnings to her sister, or of her own firm assertion that she had learned enough about the Greek male to give him a wide berth. If Adam should decide to assert his rights. . . . She, Jill, would be nothing more than a pillow friend, really, since his fiancée had first place in his life and was the one to whom he would always extend respect.

'What are you thinking, Jill?' His voice drifted to her above the chatter of two waiters talking in Greek. 'You look rather scared, and very beautiful with your colour heightened like that.'

'It was nothing,' she replied swiftly. 'Here come the lobsters!' She flicked a hand, intent on diverting Adam's attention from herself, and she succeeded. Adam transferred his attention to the two waiters coming to their table, one with the lobsters, the other with the wine, a native white with shimmering gold bubbles and an aroma that was heady.

'It was very good, yes?' the waiter said when, later, he came to take away the plates.

'*Poli kala, efkharisto,* Stamatis.'

'It is the strawberries that you have ordered for dessert, yes?'

'That is right.'

The waiter appeared with a large bowl of tiny strawberries marinated in an orange liqueur. This was followed by feta cheese and delicious small biscuits. Then came coffee and a dish of sticky sweetmeats which neither Jill nor her husband touched.

'Shall we dance again?' invited Adam, standing up without waiting for Jill's reply and buttoning his white linen jacket.

She rose and glided into his arms and away from the table in one swirling, elegant move. Others watched them, an arrestingly attractive couple whose steps suited so well that they might have been one person. Jill again felt the prickle of excitement—and fear—that had come over her before. Every sense seemed to be alert to her husband's nearness, his magnetic personality, his hard and virile body pressing close to hers as they danced.

At last they were on their way back to the villa, Adam driving in the moonlight, passing through avenues of olive trees and carobs, with asphodels flaring by the roadside, delicate ghosts caught in the headlights' silver glare. The road was smooth, the car engine almost noiseless. The sea was darkly nebulous in the distance, but foam-flecked as it touched the shore. On the far horizon several lights glittered, and in the deep purple Grecian sky a myriad of stars twinkled, a galaxy of flawless white diamonds. In the car was only silence. Jill wondered where her husband's thoughts were and wished she could read them. They reached the villa at last, its many outside lights aglow, illuminating the garden, the fountain in the courtyard and the flowers on the patio.

'Good night, my dear. . . .' Adam's voice was low as he spoke, when they were in the hall ready to go to their respective rooms. Jill knew a sudden dryness in her mouth, a racing in her heart. Adam was towering above her, his eyes fixed upon her upturned face, his mouth slightly open, accentuating the lower lip, strong and sensuous. The whole atmosphere seemed charged with tension; it created a powerful, mysterious spell which affected Jill's senses like a potent wine. She wanted to escape, and yet she wanted to prolong this magic interlude forever.

'I said good night,' her husband reminded her, his deep, accented voice edged with amusement. 'You're in a dream, Jill.'

She frowned, but did not know why. His words had such a prosaic ring that she was brought rudely out of the spell. 'Good night, Adam,' she returned. 'Thank you for a lovely evening.'

'Thank you, my dear. I haven't had much time to spend with you up till now—nor will I have in the near future, as I'm very busy at present. However, we must do this again before very long.' He flicked a hand to indicate that she should precede him, and she moved, turning at her bedroom door and waiting breathlessly—for what?

He smiled and went past her; she entered her room, closing her door only after hearing her husband close his.

Chapter Three

Another week sped by, with Jill's time being spent between visiting her mother-in-law and basking in the sunshine on the lawn, though each morning began with a swim in the pool or the sea, depending on how she felt. It was like marking time, she thought, always happy when the evening came and Adam was with her for dinner. Not that she was in any way bored. On the contrary, the visits to her mother-in-law were always something to which she looked forward eagerly, since the old lady seemed so happy and contented when she was with her.

But once or twice Jill found herself becoming restless, a circumstance that both troubled and vexed her. She had everything a girl could want in the way of luxurious living, so what was the reason for her restlessness?

Mrs. Doxaros obviously noticed it, and remarked that Jill was unusually quiet. 'Is Adam very busy in his study these days?'

There was no mistaking the significance of the question, and Jill was quick to set the old lady's mind at rest. 'Yes, he is, rather, but I don't mind at all. He promised that it won't be for too long. In any case, he's always with me for dinner.'

'You're a sweet child, Jill,' said Mrs. Doxaros, reassured. 'I'm indeed blessed in my old age.' A sigh of contentment issued from the parched and colourless lips. 'I shall die happy, thanks to you, my dear daughter.'

'Don't talk about dying,' protested Jill, genuinely distressed. 'You're going to live a long while yet.'

Jill reflected on this later, when, in her bedroom, she was changing for dinner. At first the one overriding thought in her mind had been that this false position she was assuming would not last very long and soon she would be free to enjoy the money her husband had promised to give her at the termination of their marriage. But now . . . A frown settled on her forehead suddenly. She was certainly not happy at the idea of the termination of the marriage. The admission staggered her, simply because she had entered into the contract without any emotion other than that of wanting to make Mrs. Doxaros happy while she lived. She had known that the situation she would be in was temporary and had accepted the divorce as a step nearer the reward which, at the time, she had regarded somewhat in the light of 'for services rendered.' Adam, open and forthright, had told her he was eventually to marry Julia, the girl who was the instrument by which his shipping line could merge with another, equally prosperous one. It was a cold and calculated business arrangement made some time ago by two ambitious men, with Julia apparently quite happy to play her own particular role, the vital link that would enable the deal to be closed.

Dejection spread into Jill's mind, and Adam, with his shrewd perception, said, as she entered the blue-and-gold salon where they usually sat with aperitifs before dinner, 'Is there something wrong, Jill?' Immaculate in an oyster-white suit of fine linen, he allowed his eyes to flicker over her lovely white-clad figure before fixing her with a penetrating stare.

She shook her head, assuming a puzzled expression. 'No, of course not, Adam. What could be wrong?'

'You're not your usual bright self,' he stated. 'I'd like to know why.' There was a sort of authoritative essence in his manner, a clear demand in his tone. Jill found herself colouring, aware that he knew she was lying when she said there was nothing wrong.

And yet, what *was* wrong? She searched her mind . . . and deliberately avoided an answer.

'I expect I'm a little tired,' she answered, hoping to convince him. 'I've probably been out in the sun too long as well.'

'I've warned you about that,' he returned admonishingly. 'You're beautifully tanned, so keep it that way. You'll peel if you're not careful.' He gave her a stern glance but said no more, merely going over to the cabinet and pouring her a drink. 'You look very lovely,' he said then, standing a short distance away, glass in hand, eyes flicking over her, taking in her dainty waist and the seductive curves of her breasts before moving to the gentle curve of her throat.

She smiled and said demurely, 'Thank you, Adam. I'm glad you like my dress.'

His lips curved in a smile of amusement. 'The dress is perfection, yes, but so is its wearer. You're an exquisitely beautiful woman, Jill . . . the most beautiful I have ever met.' His manner hitherto had for the most part been casual, but on one or two occasions recently his way with her had changed. He adopted a rather proprietorial attitude and air of authority, which reminded her of the Greek tradition of male superiority, while at the same time she found herself experiencing a little thrill of pleasure. Now as he spoke there was a pronounced alteration in his voice from what it had been before. 'I'm very glad that your sister broke her promise and that I married you instead of her.' His tone seemed to be vibrant with meaning, and she stared at him, the glass unsteady in her hand. Was he beginning to care? Jill's pulses raced at the thought, and every nerve in her body quivered. If he should come to love her. . . .

The question she had avoided answering a short while ago seeped through to her consciousness again, and this time an answer could not be avoided, simply because it was there already. She was in love with her husband, wildly, irrevocably in love with the man who had married her solely because of his deep love for his mother, the man who was already pledged to a woman with the power to double his wealth.

She lowered her face, anxious to hide her expression from his perceptive gaze. If he should come to care, then all would be well, but if not— She cut into her thoughts before she could become tormented by them, and decided to talk about his mother, whom she had seen that afternoon. As she had hoped, Adam was immediately diverted, interested as always when Jill spoke of her visits to his mother. There was no doubt about his deep love for her, and Jill knew he would suffer unbearably when eventually she died.

'Mother's a different person since you came into her life,' he said softly, with a smile that set his wife's heart jerking. 'You've done her a world of good, and I thank you for it.' Sincerity was in his voice and in those dark and deep-set eyes. His smile still hovered, and Jill's body quivered at the attractiveness of him. He had half-turned, and she saw him in profile against the muted light from the amber-tinted wall lamp above his head. In outline she saw features of a classical firmness and arrogance which reminded her of those pagan Greeks from whom the modern race had sprung. With Adam the pagan qualities seemed to be so pronounced that it had come as a shock to her when one day,

on the beach, she saw the gold crucifix he wore
on a chain round his neck. Many Greek men
wore them, but somehow a crucifix seemed
incongruous when worn by her husband.

Before Jill could make any response to what
he had said, he was speaking again, suggesting
that they take their drinks outside onto the patio,
and Jill smilingly agreed. It was an intimate,
flower-draped patio, saffron-shaded by the last
dying rays of the sun. Flower perfumes filled the
air, and from the sea the soft breeze stirred the
silvery palm fronds silhouetted against the darkening sky. Adam drew forth a chair for her and
put her drink on the small rattan table. As they
talked, the sun fell below the rim of the earth,
and for a few indescribable moments the wispy
cirrus clouds were transformed to crimson lace
floating in a sky of pink and mauve and pearly
grey. Then, suddenly, night descended, a deep
blue night, exciting and mysterious. All was still
but for the mimosa-scented breeze, all silent
but for the whisper of the leaves. Caught in
the magic that totally surrounded her, Jill felt
a strange lump in her throat, and a yearning
deep within her. She glanced at her husband
from under her dark lashes, his features set and
stern like the classical gods of old, inflexible as
the stone from which they had been so deftly
carved.

Sensing her interest, he turned toward her, his
eyes inscrutable as they roved once more over
her lovely curves. 'Yes,' he murmured in a kind
of pensive tone that made it appear he was
talking to himself, 'you're the most beautiful

woman I have ever known . . . exquisitely
beautiful. . . .'

Jill coloured delicately, confusion sweeping
over her. Shy and unsure of herself for the first
time that she could remember, she sought vainly for some fitting response, but all that she
produced was, 'I d-don't know wh-what to say—'
And then she was drawing a long breath of sheer
relief as one of the maids, Androula, appeared
on the patio to say that dinner was ready.

'Thank you, Androula; we'll be in in a few
minutes.' Adam's dark eyes never left his wife's
flushed face as he spoke, and when he rose from
the chair they were still fixed, so that she
lowered her head in the end, quite unable to
meet the stare that seemed to be inscrutable
even while a hint of mocking amusement lay in
its depth. But as he rose, he took her hand to
bring her up to her feet. The unexpected action
quite naturally added to her confusion; she
stumbled, was swiftly brought against him, and
before she even guessed his intention, she felt
the hard pressure of his lips on hers in a long and
ardent kiss.

'Oh. . . .' Every nerve quivered, every sense
was alive to the attractiveness of him, to the
contact of his hard and virile body masterfully
forcing itself against hers. She felt weak and
helpless, clinging to the lapels of his coat for no
reason at all. 'You . . . shouldn't have d-done
th-that. . . .' Her colour deepened as she realised
the ineffectiveness of a protest made as belated-
ly as this, her having offered no resistance when
he kissed her—on the contrary, she rather

thought she had reciprocated eagerly, parting her lips in obedience to the masterful demand made by his.

'Are you quite sure you are speaking the truth?' he asked, a hint of amusement in his tone. 'Can you honestly deny that you wanted me to kiss you?'

Jill went hot all over at his keen perception, for the question was in effect a statement—one which was perfectly true: she *had* wanted him to kiss her. But she resented his air of confidence, his amusement at her protest, and as a result she found anger welling up within her, and with it returned some measure of the self-confidence which had been an important part of her make-up since the death of her parents.

Having freed herself from his arms, she looked up at him and said coldly, 'We made a pact, Adam, and you've broken it—'

'Broken it?' He slanted an eyebrow fractionally. 'By one kiss? My dear Jill, you're being childishly absurd. You enjoyed it as much as I. We're husband and wife, so surely a kiss is permissible?'

She looked swiftly at him, her emotions all awry, as she convinced herself one moment that it was possible that he could come to care for her, while the next she was reminded of his pact with Julia, to whom he was betrothed in spite of his marriage to another girl. And betrothals in Greece were rarely broken.

'Adam,' she whispered, her eyes wide and bewildered, 'I don't understand you at all. What are you trying to say to me?'

A frown was her only answer for a long uneasy moment before her husband spoke. 'I find you attractive, Jill, and it would appear that you feel the same way about me. As I've just said, we're husband and wife, so there is no reason why we should not enjoy what is ours by right.' He stopped, pausing as if carefully choosing his next words. 'We can live normally for the time you are here—if the idea appeals to you, that is?'

She stared up at him. So casual his proposition—with no more emotion in his voice than if he had been remarking on the weather! Was this the approach he normally used? But no. He would have modified it owing to the fact that it was directed at the girl who was his wife! Jill had an almost irrepressible desire to laugh, and realised she was faintly hysterical, her mind unhinged momentarily by this unexpected turn of events. The feeling passed as swiftly as it came, and she was left drained, an ache in her heart that was almost physical.

'The idea . . .' Colour flooded her cheeks as she repeated the words he had used. 'If it appeals to—to me. . . .' Tears filled her eyes and she glanced away, toward the dark expanse of sea, cloudy except for the flickering lights of a liner on the horizon. 'You want me f-for your pillow friend?' she added, after clearing her throat of the hurtful little lump that had some-how lodged itself there. 'Is that what you're offering me?'

Adam frowned again, then shrugged his shoulders carelessly. 'I can't say I approve of my wife using that particular term,' he said curtly, 'but yes, that *is* what it amounts to.'

Turning to meet his gaze, Jill noticed that the finely sculptured features were tensed, as if her answer were of vital importance to their owner.

'You're so offhand about it,' she found herself saying. 'Does a situation like this mean so little to you?'

'I see no reason to become temperamental about it. After all, it's a situation that was almost bound to occur, wasn't it?'

'I don't agree.' Jill turned away, determined to hide her expression from him, because surely he would learn that she cared, should he look into her eyes at this moment.

'Come on, Jill,' he said in a chiding tone. 'You're not an innocent; you must have known that temptation would come to us both sometime or other.'

'I've never given it a thought, Adam. We made a bargain, and as far as I was concerned, it was made to be kept. You asked a favour of me and I accepted what you offered in return for that favour. But now . . .' She paused, looking up into his handsome face. 'Now you want to use me, simply because I happen to be here. It saves you going out and finding someone, doesn't it?' The bitterness in her voice seemed to have escaped him, and she was glad, for it might have provided him with a clue as to her feelings for him.

'I am not intending to use you,' he denied, his voice brusque and tinged with anger. 'You're my wife, Jill, and a man cannot be accused of using his wife!'

Her heart jerked as a strange fear swept into her. For there was something about him that frightened her, a sort of subtle threat in his words, a challenge in his eyes. That he desired her went without question, and she ought to have foreseen this situation when, a few minutes previously, he had remarked—not once, but twice—on her beauty. He was all Greek, possessing the Greek male's appreciative eyes where women were concerned, and invariably admiration for beauty led to the desire to taste that beauty to the full.

'I'm not your wife in the true sense of the word,' she reminded him unnecessarily. 'Our marriage was one of convenience for us both. On my part there was the same desire for your mother's happiness and peace of mind as on yours. I felt sure you knew this was the chief factor in my decision to marry you.' He offered no comment, and she went on after a pause, 'You seem to forget, Adam, that you're engaged to someone else.'

'What has that got to do with it?' He frowned. 'Julia knows full well that I've had women friends. I explained it all to you right at the beginning.' Mingling with the impatience in his voice was an unmistakable note of persuasion, but what would his next move be if she remained adamant? He stirred on his feet, a silent reminder that he was waiting for her to speak.

'We'll keep to our bargain, Adam. If you want a . . . a diversion, then obviously, with your wide experience, you'll know how to go about finding a woman to supply your needs—'

'Don't put it like that!' he broke in wrathfully. 'You make it sound almost clinical!'

Jill's brows lifted a fraction. 'Isn't it clinical?' she inquired. 'After all, you have nothing else to offer.'

He slanted her a puzzled glance, his anger evaporating. 'What else would you expect me to offer?' he demanded curiously.

She lowered her lashes, hiding her expression from his dark, intensive scrutiny. 'Nothing,' she returned, wondering at the lack of emotion in her voice. 'Nothing at all, Adam.'

A long pause followed before he said, 'Think about my suggestion, Jill. Life is for living, remember, and although I doubt it, we could be married for some time. This situation could not possibly continue—'

'It could!' she cried. 'You made a promise!'

'Circumstances can alter people's attitudes,' he returned with a hint of asperity. 'At the time, I didn't foresee the possibility of my becoming attracted to you—'

'Desiring me, you mean,' she cut in tartly. 'Desiring my body!'

'Put it that way if you like. It adds up to the same thing: this situation can't continue.'

She stared at him, having caught the emphasis, the determination in his tone. 'What exactly have you in mind, Adam?' she asked tightly. 'If I refuse your . . . offer, is it your intention to take me by force?'

His dark eyes flashed fire, and for one disbelieving and frightened moment she thought he would slap her. But if that had been his intention, he resisted the impulse, and his voice was surprisingly mild as he said, 'Let us not discuss a situation that might never occur. Just do as I say and give my suggestion some thought.'

'*Might* never occur. . . .' Nerves quivered, then went taut. Unless she were very much mistaken, the decision would eventually be taken out of her hands. Whatever Adam wanted, he would have, whether it was with her agreement or not.

Chapter Four

Jill never mentioned the matter again, and to her surprise, neither did her husband, and with the passing of another fortnight she began to feel safe. But she did at times resent the masterful, domineering attitude which Adam occasionally adopted toward her, and she wondered how long it would be before she was impelled to remind him that he had no authority over her. A few days previously he had had some business to attend to in Athens and had taken her with him, giving her a large sum of money with which to buy clothes. At first she was reluctant to spend the money, but after a little consideration, she decided, quite reasonably, that the money was rightly hers, since she had given up her post to marry Adam and, therefore, she was entitled to an allowance from him. So she had a whole day's enjoyment at the shops, indulging in the extravagance of buying expensive and distinctive French clothes. She had bought shoes to match each dress, and the kind of underwear she had always imagined buying for her trousseau. No one was going to see it other than herself, she thought, but decided all the same that she would have some dainty undies and nightwear.

Adam's mother had been brought over for a few days, and on their return to the villa she wanted to see what Jill had bought.

'All these boxes and parcels and bags remind me of my own youth.' She smiled. 'Show me, dear, what you have in them.' She spoke in Greek, although her English was exceptionally good. 'How very happy you have made me, Jill. I could never have had a more charming daughter-in-law than you.'

Jill smiled and began to open the boxes, bringing out three evening dresses, two day dresses, a couple of pairs of slacks and some leisure wear for the garden.

'I wanted her to buy more,' said Adam, eyeing the brief shorts which Jill was holding out for his mother to take in her thin bony fingers. 'However, we can go again.'

'I don't need any more,' protested Jill. 'I don't go out, as I've said already.'

'This is nice material,' observed Mrs. Doxaros. 'And let me feel the material of that dress.'

Jill handed it over, glancing at the array of

clothes scattered about the sofa and one large easy chair.

'What's in those other boxes?' her mother-in-law wanted to know, her pale eyes expectant.

Jill hesitated, then said casually, 'Nothing important, *my mitera*. I'll take all this upstairs now.'

'Nothing important?' repeated Adam, glancing at her curiously. 'Well, let us see just the same.'

'They're . . . they're . . . only underclothes,' she said, colouring slightly and wishing she had not been tempted by the delightful undies and nightwear in cobweb nylon and lace. 'You wouldn't be interested,' she told Adam's mother.

'On the contrary, my dear, I am exceedingly interested. You see, when I was young they didn't have such delightfully brief and elegant things as they have now.'

With a sigh of resignation, Jill opened one of the boxes and brought out a nightgown of gossamer silk with three rows of ruffled net around the hem, the frills being edged with soft silver lace.

'Hmm . . .' from Adam, unexpectedly. 'Very sexy.'

Jill blushed and lowered her head to hide her embarrassment.

'And these . . .' The old lady had opened a small bag and was holding up several scraps of lace. 'My young niece maintains that only the French can create things as beautiful as this.' She fingered it for a moment and then said unexpectedly, 'You are happy with my good son, yes?'

Jill nodded her head. 'Very, *my mitera*.'

'Prettily said, my dear.' The voice was soft and gentle, the lined face that of an angel. Never had Jill met anyone as sweet as her mother-in-law, and already she was hoping that the old lady would continue to live a long time, enjoying life as she was, now that her son was married. Yet, mused Jill, her own freedom from Adam, a freedom that would be better for her than this marriage in which the love was on one side only, would come only with his mother's death. . . .

Adam took his mother home the following day and, the same evening, when they had finished dinner, he said, 'Did you consider my proposition, Jill?'

She shot him a startled glance, his question coming as a complete surprise after she had convinced herself that he had decided not to mention the matter again.

She shook her head emphatically. 'It's not worth considering, Adam. You made a promise, and I expect you to keep it.'

Adam's lips drew tight. 'I believe I told you that the promise means nothing, with circumstances as they are now—' He lifted a hand imperiously, to halt the interruption she was about to make. 'I find my wife physically attractive, and I believe the attraction is mutual. We're in an artificial situation which is a strain for us both—'

'For you, perhaps!' she flashed, fighting to

maintain her composure. 'Your assumption that I'm desperate to go to bed with a man is definitely wrong!' She was almost in tears, thinking that if only he loved her there would have been no need for this practical, cold-blooded conversation. Adam noticed her tears, and a frown touched his brow.

'I am not assuming that you're desperate to go to bed with a man,' he denied in a chill, incisive tone of voice. 'What I am saying is that you must be finding our relationship as much of a strain as I. . . .' He stopped as she began shaking her head, and after a small pause he changed the subject.

She was safe . . . but for how long?

The following day Jill was having morning coffee in a *cafeneion* down on the waterfront when one of the ferries came in, and like all the others sitting at the tables of the pavement café, she became interested in the people disembarking. Tourists, mainly, but locals too, all carrying suitcases or other luggage. One tall young man caught her attention because he resembled someone she had worked with at the office. He walked briskly across the road, looking about as if seeking a hotel. But Corina boasted only a few hotels, and all were on the other end of the island. His eye caught Jill sitting there, looking very cool and very English in her sundress of flowered cotton, her russet-brown hair gleaming in the sunshine.

He made straight for her, stopped at her table,

and asked if she knew where he could get bed and breakfast for about a week.

'The hotels are at the far end. . . .' Jill pointed to direct him.

'Shall I need a taxi?'

'With that luggage, yes, I should say so.' She was looking up into his face, noting his fair skin, his deep-set eyes and wide, good-tempered mouth. She judged his age to be around twenty-seven or twenty-eight, his height to be an inch or so less than her husband's.

'I think all the taxis have been snapped up,' he said ruefully.

She nodded her head. 'We don't have many, I'm afraid.'

'Do you mind if I sit down?'

'No, of course not.' Jill leant forward to take her handbag from the vacant chair. 'The waiters seem to be very busy now that the boat's come in.'

The young man sat down, placing his two suitcases by the table. He looked at Jill with interest, and with undisguised admiration. 'You on holiday?' he ventured after a while.

'No, I live here.'

'Lucky you! I wish I could live in Greece. I'm on an island-hopping holiday. I've visited about twenty islands already, and on this trip I'm aiming to see another six at least.'

'You've not been to Corina before, then?'

'No. I don't visit any of the islands twice. My target's a hundred, and when I've done that, I expect I shall then revisit those I like best.' He looked up as one of the white-coated waiters appeared, his olive-skinned face shiny with perspiration.

'A long cool drink, please.'

'Lemonade, yes? We grow our own lemons on Corina. This very good, I bring you big glassful!'

'It's a real scorcher today,' remarked the young man—for something to say, guessed Jill, who nodded in agreement. 'I could do with a cold shower, or a swim in the sea.'

'I hope you manage to find accommodation,' said Jill. 'We haven't many hotels here, and so they get booked up quickly, especially at this time of year.'

'I didn't really want a hotel,' he confessed. 'My funds are limited and I'd prefer a small bed-and-breakfast place, if there is one.'

'Not that I know of—unless some of the locals do that sort of thing in their homes. You could ask one of the waiters here.' She was ready to go but waited to see the result of the young man's inquiry.

As luck would have it, the proprietor was ready to take in one or two paying guests, just for some extra money for the children's clothes, he said. 'I have five,' he added with a proud smile. 'Three boys and two girls. It is good to have more of the boys.'

'No dowries to find.' The young man laughed.

'That is right, no *prika!*'

'I must go now.' Jill stood up, bade the young man good morning, and made her way from the harbour to a long narrow lane which climbed the side of the hill which led to her husband's villa. He was out when she arrived home, and

Andonys told her that he had been called away to Athens and had caught the ferry that left half an hour ago.

The ferry the young man came on, she mused, realising she had only just missed seeing Adam.

'Did he say when he would be back?'

'*Ochi,* madam, he said only that it would not be until the end of the week at least, but it might be the beginning of the next week.'

'Thank you, Andonys.'

For some reason Jill felt restless, and after a wash and a change of clothes, she decided to stroll over to her mother-in-law's. The old lady was lying down, Jill was told by a maid, and more restless than ever, Jill turned to retrace her steps and came face to face with the young man she had left only an hour and a half before.

'Well,' he said breezily, 'we meet again!'

'You've settled in your lodgings, then?'

'Yes, and it's a super place—nice white villa and patios, the usual, and spotlessly clean. And those kids of Davos' are great! I'm delighted at getting myself fixed up so cosily!'

'And now you're taking a look around, I suppose?' Jill's eyes darted to the camera slung over his shoulder.

'That's right.' He hesitated a moment, his glance going to her hands, and to the ring she wore. 'You . . . er . . . wouldn't like to stroll along with me?'

She began to shake her head, then changed her mind, welcoming the change of company. 'Yes, I'll walk with you.' She smiled. 'There isn't a lot to see on Corina. It's much like any other Greek island.'

'With nice beaches, palm trees, some archaeological sites and charming people.'

She gave a little laugh. 'You've had plenty of experience, so you should know.' They had fallen into step and were merely strolling along, not making for any specific place.

'My name's Gilbert,' he offered. 'Gilbert Dawson.'

'Mine's Jill Doxaros.'

'Doxaros!' He turned to stare at her profile. 'Your husband's Greek?'

'Yes,' she answered briefly.

'Have you been married long? I hope you don't mind my asking—but you look so very young.'

'Thanks.' She laughed. 'I'm older than I look. I've been married for three months.'

'You like it here?'

'I love it. I worked in Athens before. It's hot and sticky and overcrowded at this time of year.'

'Indeed yes! Now's the time to get away. It's good to be there in the spring, though, isn't it?'

'I loved the spring best, but the autumn's very pleasant too.'

He told her he was a schoolteacher in Birmingham but was a native of Kent. She learned that he had two sisters and one brother, that his father was in the merchant navy and his mother ran a small knitwear shop in the city.

'Kirstie, my elder sister, is doing very well at university. Phil, the other one, is a bit of a tomboy and has never attended to her lessons, so she'll be leaving school next year, when she's sixteen.'

'And your brother?'

'He's the eldest. Married and lives a couple of miles from us. He works in an insurance office.'

'I've only a sister—three years younger than I,' she told him when it came her turn to pass on information about herself. She was free and easy with him, not in the least awkward or feeling she must be reserved. 'She's going out with a young man—at least, I think she is. It might all be off—I don't know.'

Half an hour later it was time for them to go their different ways, Jill having said that her lunch would be ready. Gilbert seemed disconsolate and Jill sent him a perceptive glance, recalling that when she had first contemplated marriage to Adam it had been in her mind that she might meet a young man and fall in love with him. But now . . . She had been foolish enough to fall in love with her husband, a man who intended marrying another girl in order to bring about the business merger he so badly wanted. There was no possible chance of his ever changing his mind and making the marriage permanent, simply because love had obviously never entered into his scheme of things.

A sigh escaped her, but she was finding that her mind was quite made up about the futility of unrequited love. The sensible thing was to fight it before it became too strong for her. She thought about Adam's assertion that they would go their own ways, that he would never interfere in her activities so long as his mother did not suffer. He had not pursued the matter of a normal relationship, and she now believed he was intending to keep to the bargain he had made. That he would have pillow friends was to be expected, and the idea hurt abominably, but she was resigned, simply because she was forced to keep to her side of the bargain as well. She had realised, too, that in spite of her denial her life was in fact becoming boring lately, and she had even begun to ask herself just how long this boredom was likely to continue. She was exceedingly fond of her mother-in-law and wanted her to live for many years yet, but Jill felt that to go on like this for years and years would mean the waste of her own youth, and for the first time she was beginning to wonder what had possessed her to be swayed by that dear old lady's anxiety over her son.

Another sigh escaped her; it was not meant to be heard by her companion, and she was surprised to hear him say, a hint of anxiety in his voice, 'Is something wrong, Jill?'

'No—nothing. . . .'

'That wasn't very positive,' he observed, his shrewd eyes noting the shadows in hers.

'I suppose,' she said, fully aware of what she was doing, 'that I'm fed up with my own company.'

'Fed up—' He stopped in his tracks to stare down into her face. 'That's a strange thing to say when you're still a new bride!'

'My husband's time is occupied with his business. He's in Athens at present and won't be back until the weekend, or even later than that.'

A long pause ensued, and when Gilbert did eventually break the silence, his tone and words were hesitant. 'I'd . . . er . . . like to have dinner with you, Jill—that is, I mean, if you're lonely— because I'll be on my own, and it's no fun . . . although don't think I'm not used to it. If I choose to come on these island-hopping holidays, then it's what I must expect.' He paused, but Jill did not speak. 'I do sometimes manage to get an amiable companion, though, and so if you . . . ?' His words ended on an unspoken question and Jill's hesitation was brief, for there was no harm, none at all. Adam had his fiancée and his pillow friends. It was all very amicable and free—their attitude toward each other.

'I'd love to have dinner with you,' she said, smiling, but went on to add that she must pay for herself. He began to protest, at which Jill pointed out quite reasonably that not only was she a stranger to him but also she had plenty of money as well.

They went to a restaurant where they ate *souvlaki* and drank a local wine while watching four dancers and listening to the *bouzouki* music being played by six musicians at the far end of the restaurant. The dancers, all youths, darted and dived through the Zorba-like *syrtaki,* while afterward two older men danced the more solemn *tsamiko.* Gilbert had seen the dances many times before, but, he said, he was always intrigued by the agility of the Greek men.

'Shall we dance now?' Gilbert looked at Jill and smiled. The Greek dancers had finished their performance, and a slow foxtrot was now being played.

'Yes.' She slipped into his arms, but her thoughts strayed to her husband, and she wondered what he was doing at this time—whether he was dining and dancing with Julia or with some other woman.

'It's hot in here,' Gilbert was saying some time later, and so they went outside for a stroll along the palm-fringed, moonlit shore. Time sped on, and it was after midnight when at last they were on their way to the villa in a taxi.

'Thank you, Jill, for a wonderful evening.' There was an odd inflection in Gilbert's voice as he stood by the wrought-iron gate of the villa and said good night. 'Can we do it again, do you think?'

'Of course, Gilbert.' She was affected by his charm of manner, the spontaneity of his smile. 'I, too, have had a wonderful evening.' She smiled her good night and hurried along the drive. She felt happy because she *wanted* to see him again, and surely that was a good thing?

Sunday arrived, and still Adam had not returned. Jill dutifully visited her mother-in-law, but for the most part she had been with Gilbert every day; they explored the beaches, lunched at several different *cafeneions* and *tavernas,* dined and danced and reached the point where Jill decided to tell him the reason for her marriage and that it was to end as soon as her mother-in-law died. Naturally he was amazed at the story but obviously happy at the thought that his friendship with Jill need not end when he left the island.

'As you know,' he said one evening when they were walking along the beach after their meal, 'I was intending to have only one week here, but I'd stay on if you'd agree to go about with me.'

'I expect that's possible, Gilbert.'

'And your husband won't mind?'

'Not at all. I've explained our arrangement. We both entered into the contract in a purely businesslike way, and so we're both free to do what we like.'

'It still seems an incredible story!'

'But it's a true one.' She smiled, thinking of the part she had left out—that she had foolishly fallen in love with her husband.

Adam arrived on Monday afternoon; she had already made a date with Gilbert to dine and dance at a seafront restaurant where their table was booked. She wasted no time in telling Adam all about Gilbert—that she and he had been keeping company for almost a week and that he was thinking of staying on in Corina so that their friendship could continue.

Adam stared disbelievingly at her for several seconds, a frown creasing his brow, and Jill added swiftly, 'Gilbert knows ours isn't a proper marriage, Adam. I told him everything because of the way our friendship was developing—'

'You told him everything?' Adam looked at her as if she had taken leave of her senses. 'You told a stranger about our marriage?'

'It was necessary. Surely you can see that?'
Jill's nerves began to flutter even though she felt
she had nothing to be afraid of. In going out with
Gilbert she had done no more than take advantage of the freedom which had been agreed on at
the time she promised to marry Adam.

'Am I to understand that this is a serious
attachment?' he inquired at length. He was
eyeing her coldly, his mouth tight, his jaw
flexed.

'We've certainly become fond of each other,'
she admitted, puzzled by his manner. He
seemed to be suppressing anger, and she was
impelled to add, 'The arrangement you and I
made was that we would each be free to go our
own way.'

'So long as my mother isn't hurt,' he snapped.
'That was the condition which, it would appear,
you have forgotten.'

'I haven't forgotten anything about our agreement,' denied Jill with an indignant lift of her
chin.

'Have you visited Mother while I've been
away?' The dark Greek eyes flickered over her
from head to foot, missing nothing—the slender
lines, the seductive contours, the high, firm
breasts secured in lace that showed through the
lawnlike texture of the white blouse she was
wearing.

'Of course I've visited her—several times.' Jill
considered that she had done her duty and
resented Adam's attitude, since it was he who
had said they would each have their freedom.
'Surely you realised the possibility of my meet-

ing someone and falling in love?' She stopped rather abruptly, having caught herself in the lie, and glanced away, a catch in her heart. But determinedly she thrust out the reminder of her love for Adam, profoundly aware that it could not possibly come to anything. She *had* to forget it—to push it right out of her consciousness every time it came to the fore, because that was the only way to become heart-free again and, in consequence, to turn her full attention to the most pleasant attachment that had come into her life. Gilbert was charming to be with, an intelligent conversationalist; he was tall and good-looking and his manners were impeccable. And if she didn't love him now, well, perhaps it would come in time.

Adam was silent, an unfathomable expression on his face. Jill could not understand his manner, or the long silence which, for her, was becoming uncomfortable. He seemed to be controlling his temper with difficulty. Her hackles rose, and so did her chin, but before she had time to speak, Adam had broken the silence to say, quite firmly, that he was not going to have his mother hurt by any action of Jill's.

'She'll be heartbroken if she ever learns you're friendly with another man.' His eyes were hard, like tempered steel.

'Your mother won't know anything about it.' Jill frowned at him and added, after a slight hesitation, 'I don't care for your attitude, Adam. I'm my own mistress, remember—'

'You're my wife,' he cut in sharply, 'and as

such you will behave with an appropriate measure of discretion!'

Jill gritted her teeth, infuriated by the content of his words and the manner in which he had delivered them, in that magisterial way, his whole bearing one of arrogant domination.

She said, determined to retain her calm in spite of the anger that consumed her, 'I haven't asked you who you were with in Athens, because I don't consider I have the right, our agreement being what it is. You were probably with Julia, or you might have been with another woman. As I've said, I've not asked because it's no concern of mine.'

A silence followed, and she knew he was impressed by the quiet dignity with which her words were spoken. She looked intently at him, aware that he was still angry but, like her, was not intending to lose control.

'How long is this Gilbert staying on Corina?' he inquired at length.

'He's a schoolteacher, so he has about six weeks' vacation. He'll have another five weeks—but he might not stay that long,' she added, even though she felt almost sure that he'd stay as long as was possible, just to be with her.

'You appear to have made a good deal of progress in a very short time,' observed Adam unpleasantly.

'It was one of those things. We liked each other on sight.' Jill's lip quivered uncontrollably. The idea of her having a man friend was obviously annoying to Adam, but little did he know just how painful this conversation was to her.

'And when he's left, you'll correspond, I suppose?'

'Of course.'

'And you'll both be waiting for my mother to die.' A statement, and now his voice carried a bitter note not untinged with censure.

'I resent that!' she flashed indignantly. 'I'm no more anxious for your mother to die than you are. I've come to like and admire her; we're the best of friends, so why should I want her death?' Her colour fluctuated, the result of the angry emotion spreading over her. 'Gilbert knows how deeply attached I am to your mother, and, like me, he's resigned to our having to wait, In any case,' she added, aware that she was way ahead of the situation as it stood at present, 'we've not known one another long enough yet.'

'You say he's intending to stay here on Corina for another five weeks?'

'I said he might. His original intention was to take an island-hopping holiday, and he intended staying here for one week only.'

'But since meeting you he's decided to stay longer?'

She nodded her head, and because she still resented his attitude, she said, changing the subject. 'Did you enjoy your visit to Athens? Did you see Julia?'

'It was purely a business trip; I didn't go for enjoyment.'

'But you saw Julia?' she persisted.

'I had business with her father; I visited his

home, and naturally his daughter was there.' So matter-of-fact! And yet he was talking about the girl whom he would one day marry.

'It seems very strange to me that neither of you wants love in your lives.' It was a statement, but spoken rather breathlessly, because she was vitally aware, at this moment, of her own love for Adam.

'In Greece, arranged marriages are still common.'

'You're so coldly unemotional about it,' she said.

He looked at her, an odd expression in his eyes. 'You're a romantic, obviously,' he re-marked after a pause.

'I would like to have love in my marriage . . .' Her voice trailed off, and she shook her head in a little helpless gesture that caught and held his attention.

'That sounds as if you're not too sure about your feelings for this man you've met.'

'As I said, we haven't known each other very long. We're attracted to one another, but obvi-ously we've a long way to go yet before we're absolutely sure we can make a success of mar-riage.'

'Let us get back to the question of my mother,' said Adam impatiently. 'I can't have you going about with this man for another five weeks. Mother is bound to hear of it.'

'I can make sure we keep to the other side of the island. Gilbert and I are thinking of renting a car between us, so it'll be easy to travel farther afield than we have been doing.'

Even as she was speaking, Adam was shaking his head. 'I won't allow it, Jill—'

'Won't allow—' she exclaimed, staring in disbelief. 'Do you know what you're saying?'

'You're my wife—' began Adam, when again she interrupted him.

'In name only!'

'That,' he returned with quiet emphasis, 'can easily be rectified.'

Her eyes flew to his. 'You *must* keep to our bargain,' she cried, 'especially now that I've met Gilbert!' It was a desperate statement; she knew she had to do anything she could to keep Adam from guessing her feelings for him.

She scarcely knew what to expect—anger, mastery, or perhaps even violence. Instead he looked at her with a sudden frown and said, in the same quiet voice, 'We'll talk about it over dinner.'

'I'm dining with Gilbert. The table's booked.'

'You're not dining out this evening,' he told her inexorably. 'Phone this Gilbert and tell him that, as your husband is home, you'll have to give him a rain check.'

'I shan't!' Jill quivered from head to foot with anger. 'What's the idea—going back on the promise you made? I'd never have agreed to marry you if I'd had the slightest suspicion that you'd try to control my freedom!' And on that she left him, to go up to her room to shower and change in readiness for her evening with Gilbert.

Chapter Five

They sat under a canopy of vines looking out to
where the moon-pale sky merged imperceptibly
with the smooth, dark sea. They ate mullet
roasted with thyme and garnished with crispy
fried potatoes and salad, and washed it all down
with local red wine. *Bouzouki* music drifted out
from the room behind, and two men, linked by a
handkerchief, whirled and leaped and swooped
through the *hasapiko*, a very old Greek dance
originally performed by butchers—'the slaugh-
terers,' it meant—Gilbert smilingly told Jill, but
she knew this already.

'Have you had as pleasant an evening as I?' he
was asking much later as he drove her home in
the car he had hired a few hours earlier.

Jill nodded, feeling heady with the wine and

yet at the same time able to concentrate on what might occur when she arrived home. For Adam had been furious when she had insisted on keeping her date with Gilbert, and she rather thought he would have used force to keep her at home if such a measure had been at all possible. As it was, she expected some unpleasantness, but she had no intention of being browbeaten, of giving way to the demands which she considered unreasonable in light of the agreement they had made. She could find no excuse for Adam's attitude toward her friendship with Gilbert, especially as he was still secretly betrothed to Julia. Jill was determined to remind him of the fact that he had no authority over her whatsoever.

'The gates are open,' she heard Gilbert say as he swung off the main road into the drive which led to the villa. 'Shall I drive right in, or must I stop here?'

'You can drive right in,' she said recklessly, 'and stop at the front door.' That would let Adam see that she had no fear of him, that she intended to do exactly as she liked.

He stopped the car and they sat for fully ten minutes, talking, and when at last she was getting out, he took her in his arms and kissed her.

'Tomorrow morning at half-past ten? I'll call for you?' Earlier they had decided to go off for the day, exploring the island, having both lunch and dinner out.

'Yes, that will be fine.' Gilbert was round at her side of the car, opening the door for her. She got out, coming close against him, and it seemed the most natural thing for his arms to come about her and for her to lift her face for his kiss. When eventually they drew apart, she happened to glance toward Adam's study.

He was standing on the verandah that ran the length of his picture window, and even though it was impossible to see his expression, Jill felt sure that it was far from pleasant.

No sooner had she entered the house than he came from the door at the far end of the hall, a tall, forbidding figure, a scowl darkening his face. That black fury consumed him was evident, and despite her previous resolutions, Jill knew a fluttering of nerves, a tingle of fear affecting her spine.

'What do you mean by that exhibition outside my house?' he demanded. 'What are the servants going to think?'

'As it's after midnight, I expect they're all in bed.' Jill's voice remained calm, contrasting strongly with the movement of her fingers, nervously playing with the ends of her hair.

Adam came close, towering above her, his anger obvious in the little threads of crimson at the sides of his mouth.

'It will not happen again,' he gritted. 'Understand?'

Jill's chin lifted in a gesture of defiance. 'Are you giving me orders, Adam?' she asked.

'Exactly!'

'Then you've obviously forgotten our agreement again. I'm my own mistress, get that!' Her temper was giving her trouble, but she was determined to retain her calm. 'I've kept to the terms of that agreement by visiting your mother regularly, by playing the role of the happy bride so that she can be happy. I expect you to honour your part of the bargain and remember that I'm free to live my own life. I shall not be dictated to,' she added finally, and, brushing past him, ran up to her room, anger and resentment burning fiercely alongside an almost uncontrollable desire to weep, her love for Adam pressing to the forefront of her mind, unbearably painful in its futility.

She realised that although she had spent a wonderful day and evening with Gilbert, she was now desperately unhappy because of the friction that was growing between Adam and herself. If only his anger had stemmed from jealousy. . . . Tears sprang to her eyes and she knuckled them away, then went to the bathroom to bathe her face. She decided to shower; it was all automatic, for her whole mind was occupied with her husband and his anger. What was he doing now? What was he thinking? Perhaps he regretted his marriage—but no, Jill was very sure that his mother's happiness was still of paramount importance to him, and undoubtedly his marriage had brought both happiness and contentment to what could prove to be the last months of her life.

After the shower, she slipped between the cool white sheets, but within minutes she got up again. All was quiet, so she did not bother to put anything over her nightdress as she went down to find the book she had been reading earlier in

the week. On her return to the bedroom she
stopped abruptly just inside the door, her heart
doing a somersault as she saw Adam standing
there in a dressing gown, an expression on his
face that set every nerve in her body alert with
apprehension. Instinctively she pulled at the
ribbon which circled the neckline of her nightdress, gathering it over the graceful curves of
her breasts. She saw the sardonic twist of his
lips at the action. He said in a very soft voice,
'Close the door, Jill, and come here.'

She stood where she was, holding the book
with a hand that trembled.

'I told you to close that door.' His steely eyes
narrowed, but still she made no move to obey.
She stood framed in the open doorway, a slender
figure in gossamer nylon and lace, nervous
tension building up as she noticed the burning
desire in his eyes. His intention was all too plain.
He had previously asked her to consider a natural relationship for the period of their marriage;
now he was determined to take the matter out of
her hands, having his way whether she liked it
or not. He was all Greek at this moment, a Greek
with pagan instincts.

'Wh-what d-do you want? . . .' The question
was phrased even while she was telling herself
the answer, but she had to ask it nevertheless.
She tried to add something to it in the nature of a
protest, but her mouth was suddenly too dry for
speech and she could only stare, his hypnotic
gaze holding hers as his long, lean body came
slowly and menacingly toward her.

'You know what I want, Jill.' Soft the voice,

but anger vibrated deep within it. He was not only ready to take her for his pleasure, he was ready to take her in anger.

'Get out!' she managed, in choked accents, at last. 'This is my private bedroom and you've no right in it—' She got no further; the book dropped from her nerveless fingers as his hand closed on her wrist.

'Private!' he snarled, jerking her body and holding it close so that she felt the compelling pressure of his thighs against her, while at the same time he slammed the door closed with his foot. 'Private, did you say? We'll see about that!'

'Leave me alone!' Jill began to struggle, forcing her small fists against the rock-hard wall of his chest. 'Have you no sense of honour?'

'You're my wife,' he gritted, 'and I shall take what I'm entitled to!' Inexorable the tone; he seemed to have no compunction, no recall of the pact they had made when their marriage was first being discussed.

'You're not entitled to anything!' She struggled in earnest, all her efforts concentrated on thwarting his intentions. But the powerful hands held her with infuriating ease, crushing her to him again in ruthless domination, and when his moist lips began their sensual travels along the petal-smooth curve of her throat, she quivered involuntarily and became aware of the first hints of desire spreading through her veins.

'Let me go,' she pleaded with a little sob. 'Remember your promise.' His roving hands were like warm shock waves, quickening her own desires, and under their impact she was becoming more and more alive to the masculine attractiveness of him, the sexual drive against which she would very soon have no resistance. She felt small and weak and was angry because it was a pleasant sensation.

'Let you go?' Her husband's straight black brows lifted a fraction. 'Do you expect me to stand by while another man enjoys the pleasure of my wife?' He held her from him, his steely eyes wide and arrogant, his mouth compressed to a line so tight that it seemed the blood had left his lips altogether.

'He isn't having the "pleasure," as you term it!' Tears shone on her lashes and there was a helpless expression in her eyes. Adam watched as if fascinated as she pressed a hand to her heart; it was an instinctive movement against the pain of her unrequited love, pain that was almost physical in its intensity. 'How can *you* accuse *me* of *that!*'

Adam fell strangely silent, and as the moments passed Jill began to wonder if he would take notice of her pleading and leave her alone. But her hope was effectually crushed by his next words.

'I've already said that the life we live here, together, is a strain for us both. The fact that you've attached yourself to another man only strengthens my previous conviction that we ought to live as a normal married couple until the time comes for us to part.' His voice hurt her because it was so dispassionate, so practical, without a glimmer of emotion, much less affection. 'That unnatural life is going to be rectified,' he went on inexorably, 'tonight. You'll be glad, eventually—'

'No, I shan't! I don't want you! I'm keeping company with Gilbert now, and it would be immoral for me to sleep with another man!'

'Immoral?' Adam's brows shot up. 'Since when has it been immoral for a wife to sleep with her husband?'

'You're twisting it just to suit yourself,' she accused. Tears were running down her cheeks, but they had as little effect on him as her desperate entreaty, 'Adam . . . don't do this to me.' He made no answer, and she added, 'I have a certain loyalty toward Gilbert now—and he has certain rights. . . .' Her voice trailed away to a frightened silence as she realised how ill-chosen her words were. Adam's nostrils were flaring, and little threads of crimson were creeping up the sides of his mouth.

'Do you know what you're saying?' Losing control of his temper, he shook her unmercifully, his fingers digging into the tender flesh of her shoulders so painfully that a little moan of protest escaped her. 'You're speaking to your husband about the rights of another man— *another man!*' He shook her again, adding further bruises to her arms. 'As your husband, I am the only one who has rights—get that!' He released her and she staggered away, feebly shaking her head in bewilderment. For this paganlike fury was out of all proportion. True, he was her husband, but by their agreement he had no rights whatsoever, and he knew it. The piece of paper that was their marriage certificate meant nothing; it was her promise alone that bound her to him.

'You have no rights,' she began, but he interrupted her with an imperious flick of a hand.

'You're about to discover whether I have rights or not.' Reaching for her hand, he brought her toward him again, drawing her inexorably closer when she attempted to resist. He bent his head; she felt the heat of his mouth scorching her lips, ruthlessly grinding them apart for his tongue to enter and probe, while his hand in seductive exploration found and cupped her breast, tightly pinching the nipple to raise it to the hardness of desire. His dressing gown had come wide open, and the only barrier between his naked frame and hers was the filmy material of her nightgown.

Adam said, stepping away from her, 'Let's get rid of this encumbrance,' and before she had time to dart away, he had flicked at the ribbon she had pulled and was drawing the nightgown down from her shoulders. It fell around her feet, and he lifted her out of it, his strong fingers beneath her arms, his palms like fire against her breasts. His dressing gown was just as quickly discarded, and Jill was in his arms again, his hands on her back sliding with lingering sensuality to flatten on her soft flesh, the fingers curling to enable him to take her weight as he arched her body toward him. His lips nibbled tenderly at her earlobes and the throbbing pulse in her throat, and he whispered throaty Greek endearments to her. Her body shuddered in response to his stimulation and her breath caught on a tiny sob because she knew she was lost. Her husband's hands were surprisingly gentle on hers as they lifted them to his shoulders, to hold them there, enclosed in warmth for a moment before putting them around his neck. Her fingers automatically caressed his nape, exploring inexpertly to find sensitive places, until finally she thrust them into his hair, clutching it in a feverish outlet for emotions that were driving her to the point of complete surrender.

'Well,' he whispered in a throaty bass tone, 'do I have rights . . . ?'

'Yes, Adam. . . .' She lifted her face. The parted lips, moistly glistening, were offered in supplication and taken in triumph, his kiss more primitive, more masterful than any that had gone before, and when at last he released her mouth, it was swollen and bruised and her senses were reeling, the riotous confusion of pulses and nerves robbing her of the power of thought. She clung to his shoulders, her naked body warm and pliant, while his hands continued to explore and caress until she felt drugged and helpless and craving her own fulfilment.

'Let me take a good look at you, my beautiful wife. . . .' His throaty accents were the prelude to an appraisal of her body as he held her at arm's length, his dark, brooding eyes devouring every delicate line and curve, the pearly lobes above a slender waist, the agitated rise and fall of her stomach. A hand left her shoulder to enclose her breast, stroking gently and teasingly across the nipple.

Jill closed her eyes, a little moan of complete surrender issuing from her lips. 'Don't tempt me any more, Adam . . . l-love me instead.'

A low, triumphant laugh was his only response for a full minute as he continued to tantalise—with his mouth, his tongue and the roving explorations that set every sensual nerve aflame, driving her crazy with desire for him. 'Adam . . . please. . . .'

He swung her up, his hands intimate and arrogant, letting her know who was master. She stared up into his dark face, then closed her eyes and turned her head into his shoulder, her whole being lost in the sensual torpor of her own desperate need. He set her on the bed, and then she reached out to clutch his shoulders, pulling him down with urgent fingers. She felt the wild pulsing of his heart above her, the fire of his lips on her throat, heard his groans of pleasure mingling with her own when at length the volcanic outlet of their passion consumed them both.

Jill awoke to the song of birds and the sigh of the breeze in the foliage of the palms, the slender graceful fronds that swayed against a cloudless sapphire sky. The drapes were wide, and she lay there, deliberately ignoring the face on the pillow to her left. But she was vitally aware of the warm naked body lying full length against her, and the arm flung across her stomach, and eventually she did turn her head, hot blood rushing to her cheeks at the memory of last night when her husband's violent lovemak-

ing had effaced all rational thought and she had
been transported to the very heights of rapture.

A sigh escaped her. It was reasonable to
assume that from now on Adam would insist on
a normal relationship, the kind he had suggested and wanted but in which she had refused to
take part. Well, it had been forced upon her, and
she could not foresee any hope of escape until
the marriage came to an end.

Escape. . . . Did she want to escape? Raising
herself, she leant on one elbow and stared
broodingly into the face of her husband, living
again the events of last night, admitting that all
her inhibitions had dissolved as she responded
to his violent, heated lovemaking in a way she
would never have imagined possible. She felt
richer for the experience even while bitterly
resenting Adam's intention of taking her by
force. He had meant to have her, to dominate
her with his strength, to reduce her to complete
surrender with the finesse he had acquired from
previous experience. Yes, he was the perfect
lover, giving as much as he took. Jill's eyes
flickered as he moved, and she glanced away,
ashamed of the sudden dart of expectancy, the
leaping of a pulse . . . the hope that Adam would
insist on making love to her again. . . .

But he had turned, and she slid from the bed,
hastening to the chair on which her robe lay.
When she returned from a shower, the bed was
empty. She stood there, her brown eyes pensive,
her mind alive to the admission she had been
forced to make—that she was now bound to her
husband by a physical attraction for which she

despised herself. She wanted him, desperately, knew she would look forward eagerly to another night of love even while knowing that 'love' was not the right word at all, simply because there was nothing spiritual in Adam's part of their pact. He had said that life was a strain for them both, meaning, of course, that he, being a healthy virile male, needed satisfaction. She had given for love, he for relief. She shivered, feeling as if sharp icicles were torturing her, piercing her heart. A tear glistened on her lashes, and she brushed it away, determinedly turning her thoughts to Gilbert and the relationship that had been developing so smoothly, with both of them conscious of pleasurable enjoyment of the present and, perhaps, of the future as well. With Adam there was no future; their marriage had been planned to last until his mother died, and would certainly last no longer. Surely she was entitled to one friend on whom to rely?

Adam was on the verandah when she entered the breakfast room, and he turned, his eyes hooded lazily as they wandered over her in a long appraisal. She was wearing a white linen sundress, short and crisp, with midnight-blue embroidery at the waist and hem.

'Good morning, Jill,' he greeted. 'You look very smart.' There seemed to be a veiled quality in his words, and Jill looked inquiringly at him as she stepped from the room to the verandah, to stand a short distance from him.

'Thank you,' she returned briefly, her appreciative eyes taking in his immaculate appearance, for although he was in denims and an open-necked shirt, he looked inordinately distinguished and handsome. He bore that air of confidence and authority which had impressed her at first and which had now become familiar.

'Are you going to spend a few hours with Mother this morning?' His dark brown eyes moved to her hair, gleaming like chestnuts in the sunlight.

She looked squarely at him.

'I usually visit her for an hour or so in the afternoon. However, I shan't be going today.'

Adam's eyes narrowed. 'And what do you propose to do this morning?'

She now understood the veiled quality she had heard in his voice. He had known she was dressed to meet Gilbert, and was annoyed about it.

'Why the sudden interest?' she heard herself asking, depression sweeping over her at the idea of friction building up between them after the rapturous harmony of last night. True, it was only physical, but there had been no room for disunity between them then.

'Don't ask absurd questions,' he admonished. 'You know very well that I'm not going to allow you to spend all your time with this man Gilbert. You're bound to be seen, and it's inevitable that my mother will hear of it. She's going to be made even more unhappy than she was before.'

Jill's chin had lifted at the word 'allow'; anger had surged up in her, and the rest of what he said had scarcely registered.

'Adam, please don't adopt the domineering-husband attitude with me. You and I made a pact—which has been broken in part. . . .' She coloured painfully, lowering her lashes and falling silent for a second or two. 'The rest of the promises are obviously still in force, each of us having to keep to them.' Her voice was cool and steady, but in her heart there was pain. Why should she be standing here arguing when all she wanted was to go to him and put her arms around him, to kiss away his anger? Yet this stand was in the nature of self-preservation; she needed to go out with Gilbert, for if she stayed here at the villa, she would spend the entire day brooding over her unhappy state. It struck her that she was using Gilbert in a way that was not quite fair, yet on the other hand, she knew that at the back of her mind there was hope that by some miracle what she felt for Adam would fade, that somewhere along the line her head would begin to rule her heart and guide her safely across the obstacle which her love for Adam presented as she strove for happiness.

'You have obligations, Jill.' Adam's voice recalled her, and she looked at him, noting the rigid profile, the thin line of his mouth. 'When I made the pact with you, this kind of situation never occurred to me.'

'If it had, you'd have inserted conditions?' Jill's voice was tart in spite of herself.

'Of course.'

'But I could still have gone back on my word.'

'I'd not have let you!'

'But you went back on yours, Adam,' she

reminded him quietly, but if she hoped to disconcert him, she was disappointed.

His voice held no apology as he said, 'As to that, Jill, you enjoyed it equally as much as I . . . and you're not only resigned to the change in our relationship but you're quite happy about it.' In his voice there was a satirical challenge which was reflected in his expression as his dark eyes settled on her flushed face. 'Don't deny it, Jill,' he advised, 'because I'll know you're lying.'

Her colour heightened even more, and she turned from him, her eyes falling automatically to the hand that rested on the verandah rail— her left hand—with the plain gold band gleaming in the sunlight. She frowned and looked away to where the trailing bougainvillaea vines wove themselves through the trellis to scramble over the roof supports of the verandah, providing welcome shade while flaunting their glorious shades of crimson, orange and magenta. In other parts of the immaculate gardens the bougainvillaea trailed along ornamental walls, or mingled with the flaring hibiscus blossoms which formed a long hedge separating the formal garden from the *perivoli*, where the fruits of lemons and clementines shone like Christmas lanterns nestling in polished green foliage. A little quivering sigh escaped her, for, profoundly appreciative of the beauty surrounding her, she could not help feeling deep regret at the thought of leaving it.

'I see that you have no intention of denying it.' Adam's voice cut into her reverie, and she turned with a frown, his easy, urbane manner riling her. 'I see now that I ought to have taken you sooner,' he went on when she did not speak. 'You might not then have turned to this other man.'

'I didn't turn to him for anything other than companionship!' she retorted angrily.

'But you've admitted that the affair's serious.'

'It is serious, but that doesn't mean that we've . . . we've . . . Oh, let's not discuss Gilbert and me! We're spending the day together, and that's final!'

For a moment it did seem that he would lose his temper, but to Jill's surprise he turned away, and her mind carried the conviction that he was suppressing an urge to dictate to her, to adopt a proprietorial attitude, and she thought with a little flush of dejection that it would have been the most natural thing for her to accept it if only he loved her. Fleetingly, painfully, her mind wandered to Julia, and she wondered if, when she and Adam were married, they would eventually fall in love with each other. Jill could not conceive of any girl living with Adam and remaining immune to his attractions as a man. He had everything, even that certain degree of arrogance which is an essential facet of supreme masculinity.

'You're determined to flout my wishes?' Adam's question came at last, and Jill guessed at his reluctance to admit defeat, to accept his inability to dictate her actions.

'As regards my association with Gilbert, yes.'

He seemed to grit his teeth, but his voice was quietly controlled as he said, 'Then all I ask is that you be discreet. Keep well away from this area. Where are you meeting him?'

'He's coming here—at least, I'm to meet him at the entrance gates.'

'I'm not having it,' he declared, looking fixedly at her. 'You have obligations, and you'll observe them!'

She nodded, unwilling to argue with him on this particular matter simply because she fully appreciated his anxiety.

'Very well, Adam, I'll do as you say. I'll phone Gilbert after breakfast and arrange to meet him in a quiet car park we know of in town. It's at the back of a hotel. I expect I can get a bus—'

'There's no need,' he broke in tersely. 'I happen to be going into town, and I'll drop you there!'

Chapter Six

As arranged, Jill met Gilbert at the car park, but he naturally wanted to know a little more about the reason for the change in plans.

She explained, and he nodded understandingly. 'We shall have to be very careful, then.' He was at the wheel of the hired car, his alert eyes on the road ahead, where three donkeys were ambling along, tied together by a rope held by their owner, a bent old man wearing black *vraga,* which, Jill noticed as the car came close behind him, were thick with ochre-coloured dust collected from the unpaved road. It was an idyllic morning with a bright azure sky and dazzling sunshine, and in the hedgerows flowers smouldered—oleanders and hibiscus and the lovely golden cassias. Leaving the man and his donkeys behind, they climbed into the hills, where the scenery was wilder and the streams more swift-flowing, their crystal waters tumbling over rocks or dancing round deep dark potholes ground into the riverbed by the wearing activities of pebbles over countless aeons of time. They stopped at a little roadside *cafeneion* and Gilbert parked the car under the shade of a carob tree. The café tables were on a vine-covered patio and they lingered there, drinking coffee and chatting.

'Are you enjoying it?' Gilbert seemed faintly anxious, she thought, and she smiled at once to reassure him.

'Very much, Gilbert. It's such a lovely day.' She spoke the truth when she said she was enjoying it, but her undisciplined mind kept on wandering, to her husband, and to the drama of last night, and she wondered what Gilbert would have to say if she were to reveal to him the fact that Adam had insisted that their relationship become normal. She felt he would be both shocked and upset, that he might feel cheated simply because he had been assured that the marriage was nothing more than a business contract between two people who had nothing in common.

She supposed that if the affair between her and Gilbert did become serious to the point that they decided to marry, then she would tell him, but not before. Better to cross her bridges as she came to them, seeing that there was nothing to be gained in doing otherwise.

'Do you want to buy anything?' he asked later,

when they arrived at a small town where there were shops and a *taverna* where they could have a lunch of local food.

'No, nothing,' she answered, smiling. 'But what about you? Have you any souvenirs to buy?'

'Yes, for my sisters, but I haven't any ideas.' He looked at her with a wry expression on his good-humoured face. 'Can you suggest anything, Jill?'

'It just depends on whether you favour the local products or those imported especially for the tourist trade.'

'Local, I think.'

They went into a shop and came out with two silver pendants and some hand-embroidered handkerchiefs.

'I'd have liked to buy more, but funds won't allow,' Gilbert admitted ruefully.

They stayed out late, stopping at another charming little café for a meal before returning to the town, where Jill got a taxi to take her home. As she expected, Adam was still up, sitting alone on the patio, a drink in front of him on the small rattan table. In the darkness she saw only the outline of his figure, not his expression, but she did notice that he had not changed into a formal evening shirt and jacket, as he always had when she dined with him. And as she approached, drawn by some magnetic force to join him on the patio, she felt a little lump rise in her throat at the idea that he might have been lonely. They had had such pleasant evenings before the arrival of Gilbert on the scene, she recalled, with a profound sense of loss. And at the memory a sigh escaped her and she decided to go straight into the house, but Adam called to her, and she went to him, seraphic in the moonlight, her hair a glorious halo for her face. A suffusion of colour added to her beauty as she drew near and saw his eyes wandering over her, seeming to pick out every seductive curve, lingering on her breasts and slowly narrowing, while a nerve pulsated in his strong brown throat. He rose as she reached him, and already she was affected by the superlative maleness of him, the impression of a godlike being who was far above her—remote, unapproachable.

A smile fluttered at her thoughts, and he asked softly, reaching out to take her hand, 'What is it that amuses you, Jill?' He drew her to him, his hand shaped round the back of her head.

'Just a thought,' she answered, resisting the urge to press close, to put her arms about his waist.

'Tell me,' he said imperiously, as he tilted her face up with a finger beneath her chin.

She tried to shake her head, but his hand closed about her chin, preventing her from moving.

'You . . . you seemed . . . unapproachable,' she confessed with shy hesitancy. 'Sort of . . . remote.'

'I'm far from remote at this moment, Jill. No wonder you were smiling.' The alien voice vibrated, and the eyes on hers were intensely dark with the embers of latent passion. 'Where have you been until this late hour? I've been waiting for you.'

'We took a tour of some of the island's beauty spots. We stopped for lunch at a *cafeneion,* and then again, on the way back, for a late meal.'

'What else did you do?' He held her from him and his mouth was suddenly compressed. 'He kissed you, I suppose?'

'Of course—naturally he did,' she lied, and heard him grit his teeth.

'You can let one man kiss you while knowing another is soon to make love to you?'

'That isn't of my choosing,' Jill reminded him quietly, but she had flinched at his words for all that.

'You have no regrets, though,' he asserted confidently. There was a distinct challenge in his words, but, unable to lie, Jill remained silent, and after a moment his arms enclosed her, crushing her tender frame to the whipcord hardness of his, and she felt sure that he must be aware of the wild leap of her heart, the mad racing of her pulse. His mouth was hard and demanding on her lips, his body sensuous and compelling in its rhythm; soon she was returning his passion, her moist lips responding, her supple body arched in obedience to the masterful pressure of his hands sliding downward along her spine. Her arms came about his neck, her fingers with butterfly lightness caressed his nape and behind his ears, then slid down to undo the buttons of his shirt and venture inside, plunging themselves into the mass of wiry black hair. She was conscious of his ragged breathing, the violence of his heartbeats, the brutality of his hands as they crushed her tender flesh as an outlet for the passion consuming him.

'Jill,' he breathed hoarsely, 'we must go inside.'

She nodded dreamily, clinging to him, her whole body weakened by the violence of his passion.

But neither made a move; they stood there, very close, their senses hypnotised by the moon-glow and starlight, by soft balmy air perfumed with flowers and freshened by the breeze drifting in from the sea. Sounds invaded the air—cicidas in the olive trees and crickets in dark places, the call of a night bird, the melancholy strains of *bouzouki* music drifting up over the hills from some small hamlet where the *cafeneion* was still open.

In the distance, silhouetted against the deep purple sky, rose the fretted summits of the one mountain range, on top of which stood, in stark outline, the ruins of a Venetian castle. All was magic, with that soporific gentleness in the atmosphere found only on a Greek island. A deep sigh escaped her and she turned to her husband, lifting her face, touching his with a finger, shyly, impulsively, and he smiled down at her and bent his head to take her softly parted lips beneath his own, and his manner with her was infinitely gentle.

'Let's go in,' he said again, his arm coming about her waist. 'It's very late and I'm sure you're as tired as I.'

'Tired?' The word escaped before she could suppress it, and she coloured on hearing him say, 'Don't worry, my wife, I will never be too tired to make love to you.'

It was after they had made love and were lying close, the room bathed in the warm glow from the bedside lamp, that Adam asked her if she had ever been to a village wedding.

'No,' she replied. 'Working in Athens, I never got to know any villagers.'

'On Saturday, I want you to come to a wedding with me. Mother will be there, and so you must come, too. We'll be there for two days.'

Jill turned her head, dragging her mind back from the sensuous languor into which it had floated after its wild, tempestuous flight to the boundless heights of paradise.

'Who's getting married? Two days, did you say?' she added, as the fact registered.

'We're invited for the previous day's activities as well. The bride used to work for Mother as a maid, and we'll be expected to attend.' He paused, and his features hardened perceptibly. 'Tell me, do you and your Gilbert have plans?'

'I was going out with him—'

'You won't be, not on those two days,' broke in Adam inexorably. 'You'll have to put him off.'

'But . . . two days.' She frowned. In fact, she was overjoyed at the prospect of two days with Adam, but she could hardly let him see how she felt.

'Most village weddings last for three, as you probably know. Often we go just for the day of the ceremony, but for this one we're invited for the previous day too.' Something in his voice convinced her that he had manoeuvered it, and that they could have attended just for the actual wedding ceremony and the reception afterward.

'So there's no way out of it?'

His face hardened. 'Do you want to get out of it?'

She paused, vitally aware of the long hard length of his frame against her naked body, and the hand curled round her arm.

'No, Adam,' she said, 'I don't want to get out of it.'

'Then you'll make your excuses to Gilbert?'

'I shall have to. . . . ' Her voice trailed away to a frowning silence, because it was all wrong to speak of Gilbert after the glorious rapture of her interlude with Adam; her love for him was overflowing, and she hated to let anything or anyone intrude on her consciousness of it. With a little murmur of pleasure she turned to bend her body more closely to his, and her arm came around him.

His warm hands roved over her soft white flesh, from her face and throat to the tender curves of her breasts and tiny waist, moving to her stomach and lower, his fingers tantalising all the time, feather-light, then masterfully cruel, bringing her alive again to his physical magnetism, to the invincible power he had over her senses. Her breathing became erratic; his mouth was moist against her breast, the sensuous lips open wide to take their fill, the roughness of his tongue a scorching friction on the

nipple. The possessive exploration of his hands
was the stimulating heat that sent the blood
drumming in her head, dancing through her
veins. Rapture spread gently, gaining power
until spasms of ecstasy shuddered through her
body as her stormy surrender became her own
fulfilment.

On Saturday morning they set out, intending
to pick Adam's mother up on the way, but they
arrived at her home only to learn that she had
decided not to attend the preliminary celebrations, but would go only to the actual wedding on
the following day.

'So we're on our own?' Jill said when they
were back in the car. 'You still want me with
you?'

He slanted her a glance as he let in the clutch.
'Of course. What makes you ask?' His voice was
overcrisp, as though her query annoyed him. Jill
thought it might be that he'd misconstrued her
question, believing that she would have pre-
ferred to be with Gilbert, which was certainly
not so. On the contrary, she was eagerly and
excitedly looking forward to a whole day with
Adam, being glad, in one way, that her mother-
in-law had changed her mind about accompany-
ing them.

'I ask because, originally, the idea of my
coming with you was for your mother's benefit,'
she offered at length.

'That *was* the original idea,' he agreed, but
went on to point out that his wife would be
expected to accompany him anyway. 'Many of

the people there know me, and would consider it
very strange indeed if I arrived without my
wife.'

She nodded, settling back in the car with the
intention of making the most of the drive, which
was initially along the coast road, with the
Mediterranean spread out on their left in a
gleaming, unrippled expanse of aquamarine
that met the contrasting blue of a sapphire sky.
The sun was hot and fierce, setting the mountain summits aglow, lighting up the greys and
duns of the gullies, filtering through the olive
orchards that occupied the foothills. All was
tranquil and exotic, with oleanders and hibiscus
gleaming in the hedgerows, bright butterflies
among their showy blossoms.

'Are you enjoying it?' Adam's deep, resonant
voice was fringed with anxiety, and Jill wondered why.

'Yes, I'm enjoying it very much.'

After following the coast for a short while,
Adam steered the car into a narrow road and
they were soon winding their way through the
tree-lined streets of neat cubic houses whose
gardens overflowed with flowers—canna lilies
and hollyhocks, scented star jasmines, mari-
golds and geraniums, and as many varieties of
roses as would be found in any old-fashioned
English garden. A dry, meandering watercourse
could be located by the delicate pink and white
oleanders lining its banks. Whiteness predomi-
nated, the quaint little houses gleaming in the
Grecian sun, their bright blue shutters closed
against the brittle fierceness of its midday heat.

In one village that they passed through, a gigantic statue of Christ stood guard over the square where, in the *cafeneion,* a number of stocky, brown-faced men sprawled beside the pavement tables, drinking *ouzo* and playing *tavli,* while others stood behind their chairs and watched, twirling and clicking worry beads and smoking endless cigarettes.

'I can never understand why so many Greek men seem to be doing nothing with their time,' Jill commented when the village was being left behind. 'How do they make a living?'

Her husband cast her a quizzical glance as he replied, 'Their wives do all the work. You must have seen them in the fields, or tending the goats and sheep on the hills?'

'Yes—but surely the men work as well?'

'The Greek peasants are still very primitive, Jill, especially in the island villages where the influence of the West has not yet made itself felt. Women work while men idle their time away in the fashion you've just seen.'

'It makes my blood boil!'

He laughed as he slanted her a glance, and her heart seemed to turn a somersault at the sheer attractiveness of him. He was something, this husband of hers, and it would be devastating for her when the time came for them to part. Today was *now,* though, and she intended to enjoy every minute of it, for Adam was hers and hers alone, and Julia was a nebulous figure dwelling somewhere a million miles away.

'If you were born to the life, Jill,' he said, 'you'd not complain, simply because it's traditional; you wouldn't expect it to be any different.'

'The girl we're going to see,' she began, 'Marita. Will she be resigned to a life of slavery, do you think?'

'She'll know what's in store for her, yes,' he replied matter-of-factly. He slowed down to a crawl as two black-bearded priests started to cross the road.

'*Kalimera,*' they said together, lifting their hands as if in blessing.

'*Kalimera sas,*' returned Adam unsmilingly, and although he felt that Jill would understand the added word, he mentioned that it was a sign of respect which priests always got.

'Yes, I know,' she said.

A minute later an audible sigh of contentment escaped her, for she felt very happy and contented sitting here in the luxurious car, by her husband's side, and as her thoughts wandered, she went right back to where it all began, with her sister's folly and impetuosity in becoming engaged to Adam. How long ago it seemed since that night of fear when she had been kidnapped by two men who she truly believed were intending to murder her. And then the drive in the car and then the yacht, which she had been on only once since, the drive to the villa, the name 'Adam,' which had given her the clue to it all, to the mistake that had been made by the two men engaged to abduct Susie. They had recently been given full charge of the yacht, Jill had learned, and wondered what their reaction would be if and when she met them again. Propelled by a little imp of mischief, she said, turning to her husband, 'Could we take a trip on your yacht sometime, Adam?'

Swiftly he turned, and it seemed that his whole manner had changed, that life suddenly entered eyes that had been brooding and dull.

'You'd like that?' Undoubtedly his voice was eager, and she answered without a second's hesitation, a happy note in her voice, 'I'd love it, Adam.'

'And what,' he said after a pause, 'about your . . . young man?'

Gilbert! She had completely forgotten his existence!

'Er . . . well, I meant when he has gone, of course,' she stammered.

A silence followed, with a surge of dejection intruding into her happiness of a few short moments ago.

'In another five weeks' time.' His voice was edged with irony, the cause of which was beyond Jill's comprehension.

'It's only four weeks now,' she corrected him.

'A month,' he said impassively, and fell silent, concentrating on the bends in the road, the car climbing all the time. A few houses straggled along the hillsides, the well-tended gardens including a *perivoli* where figs and citrus fruits were cultivated. In the hedges wild roses flourished, their heady perfume drifting in through the open windows of the car, mingling with the intoxicating smell of rain-watered countryside, sharp and tangible. As they went higher, the vegetation became more sparse but the air was still heady with the fragrance of wild thyme, cistus, lavender and pine. Above the tree line, the rocky summits of the high massif which formed the watershed between the north and south of the island rose in stark outline. The awesome peaks, contorted by the fire that gave them birth, towered in rugged nakedness against the sapphire sky, but on the foothills below the tree line all was lush and green and breathtakingly colourful, with elegant cypresses, pencil-slim against the sky, olives with their silver-backed leaves fluttering in the breeze. Adam swung to his right and they were no longer climbing but cautiously negotiating a road that had been cut into the mountainside to link the several villages that nestled there. Every garden flaunted a luxuriant colour pattern, the pillars of their wide verandahs veiled with bougainvillaea vines, climbing passionflowers and honeysuckle.

'This is wonderful,' breathed Jill, and wished it could go on forever.

On their eventual arrival at the little mountain village of Ayios Andreas, they were immediately greeted by the bride herself, her parents, Ulysses and Thoula, her five brothers and two sisters, ranging in age from seven years to nineteen years, and about twenty aunts, uncles and cousins.

'Come for some refreshments!' invited Ulysses, grinning widely. 'We have something special for *Kyrie* and *Kyria* Adamandios!' He led the way through an army of villagers engaged in all kinds of activities in preparation for the next

day's celebrations. Some women were preparing
spits and outdoor ovens, some sweeping paths,
others coming and going from the shops, their
arms laden with baskets and bags.

'I never dreamed it would be like this!' exclaimed Jill as she and Adam followed their host
to a low cubical house with gleaming white
walls and bright, newly painted shutters. Inside,
all was strangely quiet, and after being invited
to sit down, Jill found herself presented with
some sticky black objects, a long-handled fork
and a glass of water. Adam and Ulysses were
conversing in Greek, and while she waited, not
having any idea what to do with the refreshment
that had been put before her, she let her eyes
wander around in an interested and avid examination of a room that bore no resemblance
whatsoever to any room either in her husband's
house or in his mother's. The shutters had been
closed against the hot sun, and so the room was
dim, with a clutter of bric-a-brac and flattened
cushions, religious pictures massed on every
wall, and on the high, ponderous sideboard stood
a row of ancient icons with small candles burning beside them. All was so different and intrigu-
ing; Jill had had no idea what the inside of one of
the peasant houses looked like until now.

'You not know what to do with these nuts?'
Marita, small and dainty and very tanned,
smiled shyly as she struggled with her English.

'They're Brazil nuts preserved in syrup—
shells as well as kernels,' explained Adam as,
picking up the fork, he stuck it into one of them,
dipped it into the water to get rid of the excess

syrup and handed it to her. 'You'll find it's delicious,' he assured her, and he was right.

After the refreshments, Jill and Adam were left to wander about the village. In the square the bridegroom's *koumbari*—his best men—had the mattress which they had taken from the bride's home, and were carrying it on their shoulders, laughing and cracking jokes. Other men were dancing and singing while, blaring in loud abandon over it all, was *bouzouki* music coming from several loudspeakers in the trees, where coloured lights were also fixed.

'The whole village seems to be one gay carnival!' Jill stopped and watched the activities of the men with the bed; they were laying it down on some grass, and then came the bridesmaids—eighteen in number on this occasion—who began to embellish the mattress with flowers and ribbons and other decorations which were stitched onto the sides and the corners.

'It's pagan,' she asserted, and Adam laughed.

'There are over a thousand guests,' he told her, changing the subject, then went on to explain that perhaps half of them would be related in some way to the bride. He and Jill were standing alone, watching the activities from beneath the shade of a carob tree in the orchard where the wedding feast would take place and which was, in fact, part of the *prika* supplied by Marita's father, along with a house and several other plots of land.

'I think it's crazy, the way they have to provide dowries!' Jill frowned as she spoke, thinking what an outdated custom it was.

'It's only in the villages now, where custom dies slowly. In the town, where the girls are trained for jobs and speak good English, these customs can't survive; neither the girls nor the boys will tolerate it, just as they won't tolerate arranged marriages.'

'This marriage was arranged?' Jill's eyes sought out the bride, then Thanos, the groom, who was with the black-bearded priest who had just come round for a chat and to finalise tomorrow's programme. Taller than average, Thanos wore a certain dignity which Jill liked and which reassured her that Marita would be happy. She certainly looked happy—'radiant' would be a better description, decided Jill.

'Yes, it was arranged.'

'The couple knew each other, though?'

Adam was shaking his head. 'They met for the first time a week before they were betrothed.'

'Only a week . . .' Jill was surprised.

'Yes, that's all.' Adam explained that Thanos, while on a visit to his grandmother, saw Marita with her brother, and deciding he would like to marry her, had asked his parents to arrange everything.

'It's a crazy setup,' denounced Jill. 'What about the poor girl's feelings on the matter?'

Another smile, this time a satirical curve of Adam's fine mouth. 'In Greece, my dear, the woman's wishes don't count.' He stopped and added by way of amendment, 'In the villages, I should have said. The girl is honoured when a man offers for her, because there is a real fear among young females of being left on the shelf—'

'That's an out-of-date phrase!'

'In the West, yes; but this is the East, Jill. As I was saying, these peasant girls have a fear of being left. They want the married status even though with it comes a great deal of drudgery because they not only have a baby every year but they look after the animals and they work in the fields. You've seen them, so you know.'

Jill was frowning darkly. 'And the men never work at all!'

'Some do. Those who have lemon or orange groves water them—'

'That's not work!' interrupted Jill hotly. 'At least, not like the work their wives do!'

He fell silent, his eyes wandering to the fluted summits of the mountains on the skyline, then turning to meet hers once more. 'Let's move on,' he suggested, and his hand enclosed hers, warm and strong and possessive. People came up, congratulating them on their marriage and wishing them long life and happiness.

At length they were alone again, having left the main activity behind in the village square, and a new contentment entered into Jill as she and Adam strolled along leafy lanes where colours flared, perfumes filled the air and cicadas pulsed in the olive trees. Now and then they would come upon a row of Turkish-style houses, the flowers smothering the arches, joining them in a pageant of stage settings, exotic, almost unreal in their beauty.

'It's magical!' breathed Jill. She was happy, and it showed in her eyes and the smile that lingered on her rosy lips.

'I'm glad you're enjoying it,' was all Adam said in response, and as she looked up into his masked countenance, she had the impression that he had a problem on his mind, that he was in a state of indecision, fighting something that seemed to be difficult to fight. . . .

The sudden frown that creased his brow strengthened the impression, and she murmured tentatively, 'Is something wrong, Adam?'

'Wrong?' he asked with a lift of his brows. 'What could be wrong?' Crisp the tone, and faintly arrogant. He resented the question and had no intention of answering it.

Jill fell silent, afraid of treading on dangerous ground, and after a while the conversation changed and soon they were back in the midst of the activities, with dancing and singing going on—the dances being done mainly by men alone; but one dance, the *sousta*, was danced by youths and girls; it was a playful performance, the movements almost always erotic in mood.

'All the dances puzzle me,' Jill was saying a short while later as they sat down to afternoon tea, which had been set out on the patio of Marita's dowry house, a newly built villa in the grounds of her parents' home. 'They all have meanings, I've been told.'

Adam nodded his head, explaining that the Greek dances had survived as the quintessence of Greek history; they were an expression of the treasure of the country's heritage which not one of all the various conquerors had been able to extinguish. 'Our dances will live for as long as this world exists,' he added, with a sort of fierce pride that came as a revelation to Jill, since never before had he said much about his country and its proud claim to have brought civilisation to the Western world. 'Grief and sorrow as well as joy are depicted in our dances,' he went on, speaking very quietly, as if he were indifferent to her interest, uncaring whether she heard him or not. He was lost in reflections of the glorious history of his country, and his wife might not have been there at all. 'Instinct is the basis of human functioning,' he continued, still in the same quiet, faraway tone of voice, 'with education merely an adjunct. And dancing is instinctive. . . .' His voice trailed into silence, and he said no more. But Jill had learned something about him that was inordinately attractive, and her love swelled within her until it was a physical thing that hurt because of its futility.

Chapter Seven

After the bright flood of afternoon sunshine the air became close, oppressive, and although they could have stayed to share the evening meal, Adam politely declined, saying that a meal would be prepared for them at home.

Once in the car, Jill said, darting him a sidelong glance, 'You gave me to understand that we'd be staying late.'

'I meant to, but I decided I'd rather dine at home.' Nothing more than that, but Jill's heart was light because it seemed that he wanted to be alone with her, and she was recalling once again those pleasant evenings they had spent together in the beginning of their marriage.

They drove back through olive groves and woodlands, through villages and hamlets whose bright, colour-washed houses nestled in gardens overflowing with flowers. Sunset was fast approaching, and when at length they reached the coast road, the sea was a painted mirror fringed by palms and casuarinas waving gently in the breeze. The phantom shapes of the clouds, banked motionless above the horizon, were spangled with crimson and gold and muted rose-pearl, colours stolen from the dying sun. Adam drove for another couple of miles and then turned off the road to take a much narrower lane, and Jill turned instinctively, a question in her glance. 'There's a rather nice little *taverna* along here,' Adam informed her casually, 'where we can get an excellent meal.'

'You want to eat out?' Jill felt the warm swift flow of blood through her veins. To dine out with Adam, in this romantic setting . . . 'You said there'd be a meal ready at home.'

'So I did, but I've changed my mind.' Unfathomable the tone, and Jill had the impression that he was hiding something from her, something he did not want to admit even to himself. Was he beginning to care? If so, she could understand his not wanting to admit it because of the complications it could cause regarding his plans for his marriage to Julia and the merger he wanted to effect. 'You'd like to dine out, wouldn't you?' he added, steering the car round a tight bend to bring it into the delightful little bay which Jill had already discerned through the trees. The main lights from the *taverna* shone out onto the fine ribbed sand, pink and green and amber.

'Yes,' answered Jill at once, jumping from the car as soon as he had brought it to a stop. 'What a beautiful place this is! Off the beaten track. How did you find it?'

'It's rather well-known actually,' Adam told her, easing his long, lean body from the driver's seat with a sort of feline grace. 'At this time it's always very quiet, but in about two hours' time it'll be crowded, mainly with locals. Not many tourists manage to find the Marie Monte.'

'Is that what it's called?' Jill's appreciative gaze absorbed the impressive setting of the quaint little *taverna,* right in the circle of the bay, its tables arranged beneath vine-clothed pergolas with tiny coloured lights scattered among the foliage. 'It's something out of a fairytale!' She continued to stare, thrilled by the spectacle of crimson sea and peach-tinted shore, of palm fronds alight with golden sun-glow, of mountains ranged in mauve and purple and lilac-blue. 'Oh, Adam, I'm so glad you brought me here!'

He stood beside her, tall and distinguished, his finely chiselled features an indefinable mask, an unfathomable quality in the depths of his eyes. Jill stared unblinkingly at him, vitally conscious of a tense atmosphere, of the sparks of electricity that seemed to be flashing back and forth between them. It was a profound moment, and Jill thought that if he had taken her in his arms and kissed her it would have been so right. But he merely said, an unexpected roughness in his voice, 'Come on; let's have our meal before the rush begins.'

They ate *dolmades* first, then lobster and fried potatoes, finishing off with a dessert of miniature oranges crystallised and topped with walnuts. Coffee and liqueurs followed, and they lingered over them, watching the sunset and listening to the soft, sad strains of the *bouzouki* music, which seemed to be in harmony with the last dying rays of the sun. The air all around suddenly became heady with exotic scents— musky juniper and myrtle, passionflowers and roses and night-scented stock. Not far from the shore, little fishing caiques were silent and still, as were the graceful white-sailed yachts moored to a jetty at the far end of the bay. So peaceful, so magical, and for Jill, caught in the mystery of this island of the East, there was a sort of timeless unreality about the atmosphere that seemed to penetrate into her very heart, and she glanced at her husband, a quivering rush of hope and optimism welling up within her, for surely he, too, was affected by it all, by the romance of the situation and the setting.

They came away from the café at last, and to Jill's delight Adam suggested a stroll along the beach. To her further delight, he took her hand in his, curling his fingers around it in a possessive, masterful way. Darkness had fallen, with moon and stars taking over to provide a silver light where gold had been so short a time ago.

'This is a wonderful island.' Jill's words came softly, tenderly, and she felt his hand tighten, his fingers sliding between hers. 'I shall miss it when I leave.' She hadn't really meant to say anything like that; it came to her lips unbidden, and she looked up at him, unaware of the appeal in her eyes, of the convulsive movement of her lips.

'You'll not be leaving yet,' he prophesied. 'Mother's health is giving me no cause for anxiety at present.'

'She's happy, that's why.'

Adam nodded in agreement. 'Thanks to you, Jill,' was his quiet rejoinder. 'I rather think she would not have been quite so happy if I had married your sister.' So dispassionate was the tone in which he spoke about marriage that Jill's spirits sank, her optimism dissolved by his attitude of indifference. Wishful thinking would get her nowhere, and she must discipline herself, concentrating on what was possible rather than yearning for something totally out of reach. The sooner she fixed it in her mind that Adam would never let anything change his plans for the merger, the better off she would be. Besides, she had lived in Greece long enough to know that the engagement pact, cemented by a solemn church service attended only by close relatives, was almost as binding as the actual marriage itself. Neither Adam nor Julia would ever break it.

'Shall we turn back?' Jill's voice was flat; she wanted to get home, away from this scene of magic and romance. 'It must be getting late.'

'You know very well it isn't late,' returned Adam in some surprise. 'Don't you like being out here?'

'I . . .' Tears were close, and for the first time she found herself wondering how long she could stay with her husband, loving him as she did, knowing he would never love her. 'I feel rather tired, Adam.'

'Very well.' They had reached the end of the bay, where further progress was blocked by a rocky cliff jutting out into the sea. Instead of turning immediately, Adam stood looking down at her for a long moment in silence before saying, 'What is it, Jill?'

She glanced around, and the words she uttered came before she could stop them. 'The magic of it all, Adam. It . . . it does things to you—to m-me, I mean . . .' Her voice trailed away on a husky note as she glanced around again, every cell in her body alive to the romantic atmosphere—the solemn silence broken only by the lapping of the waves on the sand, and the music, soft and almost indistinct, drifting out from the café. The air was fresh and sweet along the shore, the silhouettes of the palms clean and vivid against the moon-flushed sky. The solitude was absolute, the tranquillity complete. Jill stared up into her husband's face and wondered why it appeared so grim. 'I'm just affected by this place,' she went on apologetically. 'Take no notice of me.'

'Do you suppose that I am not affected too?' he asked, amazing her.

'Are you affected, Adam? Do you find it . . . compelling, sort of?'

'I certainly feel compelled to kiss you,' he stated, and promptly drew her into his arms, pulling her close against the hardness of his chest. His lips found hers, gently lubricating as they moved slowly, sensuously over hers. She lifted her arms to slide them round his neck, succumbing to the delightful languor of mind-resting, while her love swelled within her and she was sad because she dared not tell him about it.

His kisses became more ardent, his hands rovingly possessive, and she was lost in a whirl-pool of passion that was as savage as it was tender.

'I wonder if you know just what you do to me?' Adam's voice was hoarse, throaty, his breathing uneven; she could feel the mad pulsation of his heartbeats and wondered if he could feel the throbbing intensity of her own heart. 'Let's go home,' he whispered against her throat. 'This is no place to be when we're both feeling like this.'

Jill quivered against him, then drew away, her love a fiery furnace, scorching her, unbeara-ble. Her eyes were far too bright as they stared into his, but either he did not see or he chose to ignore the evidence of an emotion that was outside her passion, even though related to it.

'Yes,' she returned in a rather flat little voice, 'let's go home.'

They were on their way very early the follow-ing morning, Adam's mother having telephoned the previous night to say she had decided not to attend the wedding after all. Adam was trou-bled, as was to be expected, but she immediately reassured him. She was quite well, but suffering

a little from the heat, and so she had wisely
elected to stay indoors and take advantage of the
air-conditioning.

Dawn had streaked across the sky as Jill and
Adam were having breakfast, and the landscape
was still a panoply of matchless beauty, a mosa-
ic of colour and form, with the air crystal clear
and the roads almost free of traffic.

'It's like having the world all to ourselves!'
exclaimed Jill, feeling happy at the prospect of
another day with her husband. He seemed to be
all hers, at least for a few hours, and she was
determined to make the most of it. A smile had
touched the corners of his mouth at her words,
and her heart leapt at the attractiveness of him,
as it invariably did when he smiled or laughed.

'It's certainly very pleasant to drive at this
time of the day.' Adam was sitting totally relaxed at the wheel of the car, following the same
route as yesterday.

On their arrival at the village, Jill made a
swift survey of the activities, which were in full
swing already, as the ceremony was set for
eleven o'clock. The black-bearded priest had
arrived and was performing the age-old tradition of shaving the bridegroom for the last time
as a single man.

'Did you know of this custom?' asked Adam.

Jill shook her head. 'No; it's all novel and
extremely interesting to me.'

The bridesmaids had been finishing the deco-
rating of the mattress, and now they were
trouping off to get the bride ready for the ceremony. The bride's father appeared and stood

looking down at the mattress. Meanwhile, the shaving finished, the *koumbari,* making a great deal of noise, accompanied the groom to the house of his grandmother, where he would get dressed to go to church.

'What are they going to do now?' Jill's eyes were wide with puzzlement, for a baby was being carried toward the mattress.

'They're going to bounce the poor little fellow on it,' Adam laughed. 'Wait for his protests. Our children can bellow, as you must already know. It has to be a boy, by the way.'

And he did scream, but everyone else laughed. 'Poor little thing!'

'He likes it!' said someone. 'It is for fertility!'

'It's all very Eastern,' commented Jill a few minutes later, when, money having been sprinkled on the mattress, it was rolled up and the bride's father heaved it onto his shoulder and carried it to the dowry house, followed by laughter and noise and a hundred or more tramping feet.

'There's something charming about it all, though,' was Adam's comment. 'Too many of the old customs are being lost nowadays.'

Jill said nothing, and soon the actual bridal procession was forming, the radiant bride carrying flowers, her bridesmaids holding enormous candles decorated with wide ribbon bows. The actual ceremony was hilarious, the service being repeatedly brought to a stop by people wanting to take snapshots. The smiling priest always obliged, standing between the couple, posing over and over again while cameras clicked from all over the church. People talked throughout the ceremony, and Jill thought that few had really heard anything of the actual service. At the end a wide ribbon was passed from one of the best men to another until they had all signed it. It would be kept as a souvenir by the couple.

The banquet was set out on long trestle tables beneath the citrus trees in the orchard, but at first the couple took no part. Afterward, they distributed wedding biscuits to the guests; then began the ritual dance, when the guests came forward one by one to pin money on the couple's clothes. The dancing went on for some time, until, by the time it was finished, their clothes were almost covered with paper money. Finally the bridegroom thanked the guests for coming, and soon after that Jill and Adam left.

'What a day!' she exclaimed. 'And what a mountain of presents they had!'

'A roomful.'

'Yes, I know. They couldn't put them all on display.'

'From what I saw, they hadn't unpacked half of them.'

'I wouldn't have missed it for anything.'

Her husband slanted her a glance. 'Not even for a day out with your . . . er . . . Gilbert?' he asked sardonically.

She shook her head, but frowned too, not at all happy at the way the introduction of Gilbert into the conversation had broken the tranquillity between them.

'What did you do with yourself?' Jill asked Gilbert when, the following morning, they met at the car park.

'I went to the archaeological site at the end of the island and collected some potsherds to take back to school. I shall probably do a project on archaeology when I get back.' Gilbert was driving the car toward one of the white-sanded beaches where he and Jill were going to spend the morning swimming and sunbathing. She was restless, her thoughts repeatedly returning to the past two days and the pleasure of being with her husband. Was it wise to stay with him? she asked herself. Her love was strengthening with every day that passed, and the longer she stayed, the worse the break was going to be. Yet how could she leave when Mrs. Doxaros' happiness depended on her staying?

She closed her eyes, leant back against the upholstery of the car, and tried to relax even while her subconscious was all the time insisting that she face her problems and try to find a solution. There was no solution, she decided dejectedly; she had made a pact and must keep to it. It was inevitable that Gilbert should notice her brooding silence, and he asked what was the matter.

'Nothing,' she replied, trying to sound convincing.

'You're different,' he declared.

'It was a tiring two days,' she began, then stopped, guiltily aware that she was lying.

'Tiring? Didn't you enjoy it?'

'Oh, yes, I enjoyed it. Have you ever been to a village wedding, Gilbert?'

'No, never. I'd very much have liked to go to that one, but of course I didn't know anyone who might have got me an invitation.' He was driving along a narrow lane where the land on either side was covered with undergrowth, clustering in dense luxuriance among tall palms and cypresses.

'It was very interesting.' Jill proceeded to describe all that had gone on, noticing that Gilbert nodded now and then as if some of what she was relating was known to him already. As she talked, she found herself becoming more relaxed, and after the morning on the beach her problems seemed smaller and she was able to enjoy her day out with Gilbert. They visited a Roman villa, where he took several snapshots of the beautiful mosaics that dated back to the second century B.C.; then he and Jill wandered about the ruins, sitting down for a while in one of the three atriums which had been embellished with flowers in huge stone jars and by bougainvillaea vines climbing around the columns.

'Isn't it peaceful?' Gilbert turned to Jill and took her hand. 'We're alone here, so I'm going to kiss you.' He smiled. His lips found hers in a long and tender kiss; she tried to reciprocate even while hating herself for being insincere, all her thoughts with Adam, whose kisses were rarely gentle simply because he did not love her but took what he wanted merely for sexual pleasure. Gilbert's arms came around her, and she looked down, unwilling to meet his eyes. 'Jill, dear,' he said in a quiet but tensely impatient voice, 'this can't go on.'

'What do you mean?' She drew away, her big eyes searching, a little fearful as she waited for his reply.

'I love you, Jill, and I know you love me. How long do we have to wait? I want to be with you always, even though we can't be married yet—'

'We haven't even discussed marriage,' broke in Jill in a distressed little voice. 'We must get to know each other better first.'

'I've just said I love you,' he reminded her quietly.

She fell silent, wishing he had not said he loved her. It was too soon; he was going far too fast for her. She felt his arms come about her again, made no protest when he kissed her cheek, then turned her face toward him to take her lips.

'Can you honestly say that marriage to me has never occurred to you?' he asked when he had released her. She looked at him through troubled eyes, caution restraining her from giving a truthful answer, as she felt that, if he were absolutely sure of her, he would not hesitate to go to Adam and put the whole situation before him.

'I can't be thinking of marriage to one man while I'm married to another,' she said at last in low, complaining tones which she hoped would deter him from pursuing the matter.

'You're not really married to him,' stated Gilbert, not intending to be put off. 'It's a marriage in name only and can easily be annulled.'

A marriage in name only. . . . How little he knew! He seemed so complacent about it that Jill was almost impelled to tell him the truth. But she refrained, unwilling to face what would follow a confession like that. Gilbert might be so angry that he would throw her over—but no; he loved her too much for that. He'd be upset, though, and everything would be spoiled. If only Gilbert could have left things as they were. She needed a friend right now, and for her, Gilbert had been that friend, although in his own mind he had been so much more.

'You're forgetting the main point of my marriage, Gilbert,' Jill said at length. 'I married Adam so that his mother would die happy. I can't go back on the bargain I have made; my conscience wouldn't let me even if I wanted to.'

He looked squarely at her. 'You sound as if you don't want to, which doesn't make much sense to me. Surely you want your freedom?'

'Sometime, yes, but when I agreed to marry Adam, I didn't expect to be free in a few weeks.'

'How long, then?' he asked, and a frown came suddenly to Jill's wide brow.

'I can't wish death on anyone,' she said sharply. 'That would be inhuman.'

A sigh escaped him, and he sat in brooding silence for fully sixty seconds. 'I didn't expect my feelings for you to develop as quickly as this, Jill, but they have. I love you to distraction, and the thought of having to wait indefinitely is already unbearable, so what I shall feel like when it's time for me to leave here, I don't know.'

'We still have three weeks,' she reminded him, forcing a smile to her lips. 'Let's make up our minds to enjoy our time together.'

He smiled then, and brushed her lips with his own. 'All right, darling. Forgive me for troubling you like this. I do understand, but I'm impatient, too, because I can't imagine life without you.'

Chapter Eight

It was only three days later that Adam said, his eyes deliberately avoiding those of his wife, 'Mother wants to go to Athens, so I'm taking her in the yacht. She won't fly—but you know that.' A small pause before she heard him add, 'You will have to come, too, Jill. You do understand why?'

She shot him an accusing glance. 'Must I? What about Gilbert?'

Adam's eyes narrowed. 'Surely my mother is of greater importance than Gilbert? After all, he knows you're married—'

'I told you, Adam, that he knows everything— that our marriage means nothing.'

'He knows *everything*?' repeated Adam slowly, a stress on the last word.

Jill coloured. 'No, not everything,' she returned quietly.

Adam stared down into her pale face. 'Tell him why you have to come with me. He'll understand.'

'And if he doesn't?' she flashed, anger rising at Adam's indifferent manner.

'Then it's just too bad.' Adam lifted a hand to stifle a yawn, and Jill's anger grew. 'Your first duty is to me, with whom you made a bargain—'

'Which you didn't honour!' she flashed.

'Shall we keep to the point, Jill? As I said, your first duty is to me. You promised never to do anything that might upset my mother, and therefore, you must be ready to make sacrifices.'

'It seems strange that your mother wants to go to Athens.'

'It's not strange at all. She came for our wedding.'

'That was different. She's not well, and she's old. I should have thought she'd rather stay at home.'

'We'll be away for about four days,' Adam said, ignoring her words. 'Mother wants to visit some friends, so we shall be in the city for at least two nights, but probably three.'

Jill looked away, a feeling of defeat and desolation sweeping over her. She *was* sorry for Gilbert, of course; it didn't seem fair to leave him alone again so soon. But most of all she was afraid, afraid that after another few days in her husband's company she would never be able to live without him, never be able to hide her true feelings from him.

'I don't think you ought to have agreed to take your mother to Athens at this time,' she said with a sigh. 'We could have taken her later, when Gilbert has left.'

'It so happens that she wants to go now. I was going on business anyway, and so she decided to come along, too.'

Jill looked suspiciously at him, wondering if he had arranged it deliberately just to keep her away from Gilbert. 'When are we to go?' she asked after a long silence during which she sought for some way she could avoid going with him.

'Tomorrow.'

Her eyes widened. 'Tomorrow? You haven't given me much warning!'

'My business is urgent,' replied Adam in hard and lofty tones, 'as it very often is. I travel regularly between here and the capital, as you very well know.'

She looked at him, suspicion still in her eyes. But she could read nothing in the dark mask of his face, the cold impersonal look in his eyes.

'I'll tell Gilbert today, then,' she said. 'It's a shame that he's being left on his own like this, because it was in order to be with me that he changed his original plans.'

Adam said nothing; he was not in the least interested, and as soon as breakfast was over he left her with the reminder that they would be leaving very early the following morning.

The tang of the sea, the smooth progress of the yacht over the aquamarine waters, the luxuri-

ous loungers on the sun deck—all these could
have contributed to a situation that was heaven-
ly if only Adam had cared, if he were here beside
her, relaxing in the sunshine. But he was in one
of the cabins, working, while his mother was
lying down, saying she was tired as a result of
not sleeping the night before. Jill had been
worried about her, and watching Adam's face
when his mother announced her intention of
lying down, knew that he was worried too.

Jill sipped an iced lemonade through a straw;
the drink had been brought to her by Petros,
whose whole manner was apologetic. Jill had
not forgiven him, though, and he received no
response to the smile he gave her on placing the
glass of lemonade in front of her. Georgios was
at the wheel, singing a Greek song that was
sweeping the country at the present time.

Inevitably, Jill's thoughts returned repeatedly
to Gilbert's reaction to the information that,
once again, he would have to be left on his own.
He had been more angry than Jill would ever
have expected him to be, and he had been
determined at first to go to Adam and discuss
the position with him, explaining that the affair
between him and Jill was serious. It had taken
all Jill's efforts at persuasion to stop him, and in
fact she was in tears before he finally gave in.
She didn't want to think about how Adam would
react if Gilbert did confront him, or of how such
a confrontation would affect her. She loved her
husband, and wanted to stay with him for as
long as she could. And she knew she could never
have a future with Gilbert after having loved

Adam. He would have to accept her as a friend or not at all. She knew that a future with Gilbert would be safe and secure, but it was a future she wouldn't have and didn't want. But she wished she knew what her future *would* be, for as she had told herself many times before, there was no future for her with her husband. Tears suddenly filmed her eyes at this reminder, which came to her so very often, and she was brushing them away when Adam appeared, his eyes narrowing instantly, his voice hard and cold as he said, 'Crying for Gilbert, are you?'

She shook her head abstractedly, her whole being affected by the sheer perfection of the picture he made—the burnt-sienna skin tightly drawn over high cheekbones, the fine, nobly chiselled jaw and chin, the mouth, sensuous, with the lower lip protruding slightly beyond the top one. She looked at his dark hands, muscular and sensitive, like a surgeon's or a pianist's.

'No,' she answered, 'I'm not crying for Gilbert at all.'

He sat down on the spare lounger. 'Why the tears, then?' His eyes swept her near-naked figure, taking in the gleaming honey-tan, the slender limbs and tiny waist, the firm high breasts half-revealed by the scantiness of the bikini she was wearing. 'No one cries for nothing.'

'I wasn't really crying,' she denied, yet unconsciously brushed a hand over her eyes again.

'You'd obviously rather be with him, though.' Adam's voice carried an odd sort of ring which

Jill wished she could understand. He seemed to be probing, deeply intent on the answer she would give. And because she could not produce the truthful answer, she said yes, she would rather be with Gilbert.

'He's in love with me,' she added, and in her voice there lay defiance, because she was suddenly terribly afraid that her husband, with his keen perception, might just guess that she had foolishly fallen in love with him. She was not willing to suffer such humiliation, and so she added, still with that same element of defiance, 'He was very angry at my having to leave him, and I agreed with him that it was wrong of you to dictate to me.'

'Did I dictate?' Low the tone, and somehow dangerous. Jill felt tingles along her spine; she didn't care for Adam's expression any more than she cared for his voice.

'Yes,' she replied at length, 'you did. You always do,' she added, just for good measure.

'You *do* happen to be my wife,' he told her harshly. 'And while you are, you'll adhere to my wishes!'

Jill flashed him a glance, her mouth tight. 'You didn't tell me that when you were trying to persuade me to marry you!'

'I'm not intending to quarrel with you,' gritted her husband. 'Just keep in mind that my wishes come before anyone else's.'

'Including my own?' She was quivering with anger, her eyes darting to the door through which Mrs. Doxaros would come if she decided she had had sufficient rest. Jill had no wish for her mother-in-law to witness this little scene, for it would upset her dreadfully.

'Including your own!' snapped Adam, and left her.

Her angry eyes followed his tall figure as he went over to talk to Petros, giving him some instructions. A short while later lunch was served in the saloon, but Mrs. Doxaros remained in her cabin.

'She isn't well, Adam.' Jill looked anxiously at him, all her anger forgotten. 'I'm worried about her.'

'So am I.' This was said tersely, with a most odd inflection in his voice. 'Perhaps I ought not to have pandered to her and let her come with me.'

Jill looked intently at him but said nothing. If his mother had not come, then there would have been no need for Jill to come either. Had he arranged it, as she suspected, in order to keep her away from Gilbert? If so, and anything happened to his mother, he wasn't going to feel very happy about it, that was for sure.

Lunch was a silent meal, but to their relief, Mrs. Doxaros appeared soon after it was over and was persuaded to have some sandwiches and coffee.

'Are you sure you're not ill?' Adam's eyes were searching, his voice edged with concern. 'You're pale . . .' His voice trailed off as she shook her head.

'I'm not ill, Adam,' she said in Greek. 'You fuss too much, dear.'

He smiled then, and Jill caught her breath at the tenderness of his face. If only he would look at her like that!

Wishful thinking again; the sooner she stopped it, the better off she would be.

The yacht reached Piraeus at five o'clock that afternoon; Adam had a hired car waiting, and they were driven to the flat, where, later, they dined and Mrs. Doxaros went to bed early.

'How about an hour or two in the city?' Adam inquired of his wife. 'The night's young yet.'

Jill nodded her agreement at once, for she loved Athens, being familiar with the streets and buildings and, of course, the fantastic antiquities, of which there were many in addition to the beauty and impressiveness of the Acropolis.

'Your mother will be all right, won't she?' Adam had a middle-aged couple living permanently at the flat, which was one of the largest in the tall, luxurious block overlooking Syntagma Square, where the former Royal Palace was also situated. This couple, Charon and Rita Tombasis, looked after the flat, and so it was always ready whenever Adam wanted to stay there.

'Of course.' Adam was in a white safari suit, tall, distinguished, full of self-confidence and faintly arrogant, his dark eyes moving from Jill's face to her figure, taking in the slender lines beneath the pure silk trouser suit she wore, the delicate curves of waist and hips. 'You're very beautiful,' he said unexpectedly, and kissed her. She coloured, lowering her long curling lashes to hide her expression.

'Thank you, Adam,' she murmured shyly, and heard a low laugh escape him.

'Very prim all at once,' he remarked, but that was all. His manner had changed with an abruptness that shocked her. He seemed to frown, to be admonishing himself for something. As on several similar occasions recently, Jill would have given much to read his thoughts.

After descending in the lift, they were soon crossing the square, so well-known to Jill with its luxury hotels, its outdoor cafés, its newspaper kiosks and shoeshine boys. It was always a noisy city, with police whistles heard all the time as traffic and people were controlled. High on its sacred rock was the Parthenon, and other famous buildings, all illuminated as the spectacle of the *Son et Lumière* was being presented for the tourists.

'I love it best at sunset,' Jill said as they strolled along. 'The mountains turn to a fantastic transparent purple and it seems to radiate right over the waters of the gulf.'

'Yes, you're quite right, it does. You can notice it, too, on the peak of the island of Aegina.'

'There's no city in the world like Athens,' she declared enthusiastically, and Adam turned his head, a curious expression in his eyes.

'It's just struck me how little I know about you. How did you come to be in Athens in the first place?'

She told him, slanting him an upward glance, puzzled by his manner, his interest after all this time. Right at the start he had said that it wasn't

necessary for them to go into details about the
past; their marriage was just a business deal
which was temporary, and when it was dissolved they would probably never see each other
again.

'You'll miss it when you return to England,' he
commented, a rough edge to his voice.

'Yes, I shall.'

'I suppose Gilbert wants you to return to
England as soon as you're free?' They were at
the edge of the pavement, held up by the policeman in control of the traffic.

'He'd like me to go back with him—' She
stopped, not having meant to mention anything
like that.

'But you wouldn't?' Sharp his voice, imperiously masterful. 'You're my wife, and until
something happens to my mother, you'll remain
with me.'

She looked at him, under no illusions as to the
immense sexual stimulus of her attraction for
him. She strongly suspected that he was already
thinking about what he would lose when at
length she was free to leave him.

'I shall not do anything to upset your mother,'
was her softly spoken rejoinder. 'I made a pact
which I intend to keep, no matter what happens.' Steadfast the tone, and in her eyes a
sincerity that caught and held his attention; she
saw him eventually lower his lids as if he would
prevent her from reading his expression. It was
a tense moment, with strange, inexplicable
vibrations passing between them. Jill waited, a
little breathlessly, for him to speak, sensing that

something momentous was about to happen.
But the policeman's whistle shattered the impression, and she sagged with disappointment
even while searching her mind for a reason why
she had been so expectant. He had taken her
arm as they went with the mob pressing forth to
cross the road before the whistle pierced the air
again, and had apparently forgotten what he
was going to say.

'Let's go to the hill of Lycabettus and look at
the view,' Adam suggested when they had
reached the pavement again. 'You've been up
there, of course?'

She nodded, recalling her wonderment the
first time she viewed the city at night from the
famous hill. She had just stared in stupefaction
at the incredible panorama of a million city
lights, all colours, glittering like stars in a dark
sky.

'Yes, several times, but it is a spectacle you
can see over and over again and never tire of.'

Later, when they were there, standing by
themselves in the shadow of a cypress, looking
down at the fantastic sight, she felt her husband's arm come about her waist, and automatically she pressed her slender body against him,
vitally alive to the pull of his magnetism, to the
musky male smell of him, the warmth of his
hand through the material of the blouse top of
the suit, its strength as he pressed his fingers
possessively into her waist. She felt small beside
him, weak, submissive, and she lifted her face,
inviting his kiss. For a long tense moment they
stared into each other's eyes, and then he bent

his head and took her lips beneath his own. Her
arms came up around his neck; she caressed his
nape, behind his ears, her fingers feather-light
at first, but soon the explorations became urgent
and she realised she was fighting to bring him
more alive to her attractions than ever before,
endeavouring to make herself indispensable to
him while at the same time admitting that what
she wanted from him was something far deeper
than physical love.

'You're . . . wonderful. . . .' Sensuous lips slid
moistly over hers, fierce in their ardour, cruel in
their mastery. His strong frame crushed hers,
its coiled-spring hardness a painful stimulus
igniting her own passion, and she clung to him,
her pliant body responsive to every intimate
exploration of his lean brown fingers. Meekly
and willingly she pulled away at the insistence
of his hand seeking the buttons of her blouse;
tremors swept through her with violent intensity
when his avid mouth closed over her breast, the
tantalising roughness of his tongue a nerve-
shattering experience robbing her mind of all
rational thought, of everything except the burning desire to be possessed, bent to complete
submission by the primitive male mastery he
always exerted over her. An involuntary little
moan of protest left her lips and she buried her
face in the curve of his throat, her small hands
convulsively closing on the wiry thickness of his
hair. She felt the swift unexpected spasm that
shot through him, and the aftermath of his
wildly beating heart. They were still alone in
their small area of darkness, but otherwise there

were people about, tourists who had come up by the funicular for a panoramic view of the entire Athens basin.

'Come, my beauty,' he murmured hoarsely, and she nodded. Adam took her hand, silently they moved toward a lower slope of the hill, and then back to the city, its traffic and its noise, and then to his flat and the gentle darkness surrounding the big bed.

Chapter Nine

Early the following morning, Adam took his mother to the home of her friends, where she would stay the night. Jill went along, too, and was introduced to them, after which she and Adam left. He dropped her off in Ermou Street, where there were many luxury shops—boutiques selling the latest Paris fashions, furriers, jewellers and shoe shops.

'Have a good time,' advised Adam as she got out of the car, 'and don't spare the expense. If you want something and haven't the money, have it put aside and you can call for it tomorrow. You do have some money, though?'

'Plenty,' she assured him, excited at the idea that he was willing to buy her anything she wanted. Surely he must have some affection for her. . . .

'I'll be back at the flat around half-past six and we'll dine at the Grande Bretagne. I'm sorry my business is going to take the whole of the day, but we'll see what we can do about tomorrow. I might be able to finish by noon.' With a wave of the hand he started the car and drew away from the curb. She watched the press of vehicles close about it on the road until it disappeared, and then she turned, her mind thoughtful, her memories bringing back last night and the sheer beauty of their lovemaking. So tender her husband had been, despite the violence that possessed him in the end. Try as she would, Jill could not accept that Adam had felt nothing more than physical desire for her.

She sighed, though, because her mind almost instantly rejected the possibility of his falling in love with her. He was a keen businessman with plans for making substantial additions to his already vast financial empire, so it was most unlikely that he would complicate it all by falling in love. Besides, hadn't he said, right at the beginning, that Greek men rarely fall in love? It was true; Jill had learnt a good deal while living in Athens, and she knew that very seldom was there any depth to a Greek marriage. Yet she had once heard that when a Greek man did fall in love it was forever, that he made a fiercely jealous husband who would not hesitate to punish his loved one if she should give him cause to doubt her.

Jill shuddered at the idea of being punished by

Adam, and yet, paradoxically, she would have been thrilled, deliriously happy, if, because he loved her, he had wanted to punish her. It was all extremely illogical and complicated, she thought, and let her mind dwell on her relationship with Gilbert, which, if she had been able to see it as a marriage, would be totally uncomplicated. More than ever, though, she knew that she could never marry him, could never opt for that safe, uncomplicated life. With Adam there were interludes of excitement, while life with Gilbert would be dull, with a straight-and-narrow road ahead—no turns to bring the unexpected, no ups or downs. . . .

Again she deliberately diverted her thoughts, deciding to go along to her villa, just to see if everything was all right. But when she phoned the bank to ask her friend Astera to have the key ready, she was told that the other girl was away for a fortnight on holiday. As the other key was at home, Jill had to give up the idea of entering the villa, but she did take a look at the outside before giving all her attention to her shopping. By the time she went back to the flat for lunch, she had three evening gowns, two blouses and matching skirts in fine linen, several sunsuits and a pair of evening shoes.

The taxi put her down at the entrance to the flats, and she took the lift up to Adam's apartment. After lunch she went off again, this time to look at the lovely Byzantine church of Aghios Eleutherious, built of beautiful marble which had matured from gleaming white to a glowing golden ochre. She was fascinated by the classi-

cal fragments built into the walls—pieces taken
from even older buildings than the twelfth-cen-
tury church as it stood today. From there she
went to another Byzantine church close by, the
Tower of the Winds, the church of Panaghia
Sotira, which had once been turned into a
mosque by the invading Turks, and then de-
graded to a military bakery before being restored
to the Virgin. After that Jill took a taxi back to
the flat and waited for Adam to arrive.

He was early, and they sat on the balcony
overlooking the square and watched the sunset
turning the mountains from pale gold to purple,
a sight so fascinating that Jill felt she could
never tire of the spectacle even if she were to
live in Athens all her life.

Adam had asked if she had had a good day,
and she had shown him what she had bought.
'Wear the leaf-green one,' he said, when eventually they went inside to get ready. It had no
straps, merely being kept up by soft elastic
threaded into the pleated top. She looked adora-
ble in it, the honey-tan of her skin even and
smooth, her hair gleaming, her eyes aglow. She
wore a necklace which had been her mother's—
silver with matching eardrops.

'I ought to be making love to you instead of
taking you out,' declared Adam when she stood
before him, feeling good because she was with
him and because she knew he was admiring
her, finding her exceptionally attractive. She
had coloured at his words, and he kissed her,
almost tenderly. She stared up into his dark,

brooding face, a desperate yearning in her eyes. He looked into them for a long unfathomable moment, and slowly a frown formed between his eyes.

'Let's be off,' he said, the sudden change in him staggering, for his tone was brusque, his dark eyes veiled.

They were conducted to the table which Adam had booked, and offered a menu. Someone called Adam's name, and he turned his head. Looking past him, Jill saw a tall, dark Greek girl coming toward their table; her eyes fixed on Jill for a few fleeting moments before she spoke to Adam, who had risen immediately and was smiling at the girl.

'I find you here, Adam, and yet you never told us you were to be in town.' She spoke with an accent, pronounced but attractive, and Jill guessed that she had done so for politeness, knowing Jill was English. 'How long have you been in Athens?'

'We arrived this morning. Julia, meet Jill.'

'How do you do?' The tone was condescending, the handclasp indifferent. But the dark eyes were all-examining, moving from Jill's gleaming hair to the delicate slope of her shoulders and downward as far as they could go; then they returned to her face. Jill, feeling like a piece of glass being examined for flaws, coloured and was furious because of it. 'How long are you here for, Adam?' purred the girl, turning to him again.

'Just a few days. I shall probably be seeing

your father.' His glance flicked to his wife's face, but he seemed not to notice her embarrassment, which only went to show just how casually he regarded the whole affair of his marriage to one girl while being secretly engaged to the other, thought Jill in pain. Adam looked around. 'You're not alone?'

She shook her head. 'I'm with Manos and Sophia; they're talking to a friend . . .' She flipped an elegant hand. 'Over there.' She paused a moment and then said in Greek, 'I don't think you should be bringing this woman here, Adam. After all, she is nothing—'

'I think your friends are coming,' broke in Adam. 'Which is your table?' She told him, and after murmuring an 'Excuse me' to Jill he escorted her to the table she had indicated. Jill watched them go through eyes that were brooding and dark. The girl certainly was a beauty, with flawless skin and features moulded on classical lines. She had a superb figure clothed impressively in pleated black chiffon over an underskirt of coral satin. Her hair was immaculate, coiffed in an elegant, sophisticated style with a French knot at the side. It shone, raven black, like Adam's. It seemed to Jill that he must eventually fall in love with the girl, once they were married. Yes, it could not be otherwise, she decided on seeing the girl's face again as she sat down. She was perfect . . . and she had a shipping company as a dowry. . . .

Adam made no apology as he sat down opposite his wife again; he was either not in any way troubled by Julia's words or he felt they were best ignored. But the evening was spoiled for Jill, and she was glad when it was over and they returned to the flat.

In their bedroom, she undressed while Adam was taking a shower; she did not want him to come to her, and when he returned she said she was tired. His brows lifted and he said tersely, 'Are you telling me to go into another room, Jill?'

She shrugged carelessly. 'There are two others. Yes, I would prefer to be on my own tonight, Adam, if you don't mind?' She felt like crying and thought her nerves must be on edge because of the unexpected meeting with the girl who would soon take her place.

'I do mind,' he answered softly, almost dictatorially. 'I said before we went out that I wanted to make love to you.' He paused to let her speak, but she said nothing.

Turning from him, she picked up a hairbrush, but it lay idle in her hand as she looked at him through the mirror, resentment in her eyes because she was recalling his total indifference toward the situation when Julia had come up to their table. She said at last, speaking her thoughts aloud, 'You seemed completely unaffected by Julia's appearance, not caring that I might be embarrassed.'

Adam's dark eyes narrowed. 'You forget your position,' he returned coldly. 'I won't have you taking on the attitude of a possessive wife.'

Jill's eyes widened, sparks of anger in their depths. 'You can talk like this to me, when you

yourself have adopted the attitude of a possessive husband?'

He had the grace to avoid her accusing eyes,
but when he spoke there was neither contrition
nor regret in his words. 'That's different altogether. I've asserted my rights to make things
easier for us both, because, as I said, we were
living under a strain—'

'*You* were living under a strain,' she broke in,
enraged. 'Why didn't you go out and find a pillow
friend? I'd have liked that a lot better!'

'Liar,' he threw at her contemptuously. 'It's
just like a woman to put on a pretence like that.'
He paused to let her speak, but she began
brushing her hair, her cheeks colouring at the
words he had uttered. 'The indignant-maiden
attitude doesn't suit you at all,' he continued
presently, 'not in view of your extremely passionate nature.'

Her colour heightened, and so did her temper.
Swinging round, she threw the brush at him, but
he dodged it without effort and caught her wrist
before she could lower her hand again.

'Curb your temper, my fiery beauty, or I'll curb
it for you!' He jerked her with such violence that
she was momentarily robbed of breath, his arms
hawsers of steel as he put them around her. His
dark face was above hers for what seemed an
eternity before he took possession of her lips.
With fury the spur, she began to struggle, but
the results were negligible, for all she managed
was to twist her face away, freeing her mouth
from the bruising pressure of his lips. But he

gripped her face in lean brown fingers, imprisoning it even as her body was imprisoned. The intense metallic eyes were dark with anger, the mouth compressed into a thin, cruel line. Why was he so furiously angry? wondered Jill, suddenly conscious of the fact that the strength of his anger was totally out of proportion, and it struck her—although for no reason that she could explain—that Adam was as angry with himself as he was with her.

'Let go of me!' she cried, as she tried in vain to twist from the punishing grip of his fingers on her chin. 'You're . . . you're hurting me. . . .' Tears were filling her eyes, for she was suddenly enmeshed in a coil of sheer misery that seemed to be tightening all the time. She loved him so much—wanted to be pliant and meek and giving, yet here she was, forced by pride to fight him, to pretend that she did not want the passionate lovemaking that always transported her to the very heights of heaven. 'Why don't you go away when you know I don't want you?'

'You'll want me in a moment or two,' was his arrogant rejoinder as he bent to take her lips again, the moistness of his mouth a heady lubrication, his insistence a mastery she could not resist, and she parted her lips obediently, allowing his tongue to enter and explore, while his warm and dominant hands constrained her body to the same obedience as he pressed it to the teak hardness of his sinewed frame, forcing her to arch against him, to be fully aware of his need. Mastery and arrogance characterised his every move as his fingers explored, as his mouth crushed hers; he seemed not to care for her feelings, or that he was hurting her, using her for the outlet of a passion that had been partly born of anger. She wept, and the bitter tears were wet against his face; her lips implored when at last they were released from the pain that he had inflicted on them, but he was immune to any appeal she tried to make. She felt his ardour reflected in the rapid beating of his heart, the primitive way he was crushing her tender breast within his hand. She shuddered, but it was partly with the pleasure-pain of his hard body against hers, of the unbridled dominance he was exerting over her.

'And now do you still say you don't want me?' There was a distinct note of sardonic amusement in his voice, a mocking expression in his eyes, as, holding her at arm's length, he looked down into her white, tearstained face. 'Well, answer me,' he commanded, tilting her chin when she lowered her lashes.

'Why must you torture me, Adam?' So quiet her voice and gently pleading. 'I've done nothing to deserve this treatment, and you must admit it if you're honest.' She had the satisfaction of seeing him frown and catch his lower lip between his teeth. 'What did I do to anger you so much?' she added, after a long pause in which she waited for him to speak.

'For one thing, you threw that brush at me. . . .' His finely timbred voice trailed off into silence, and Jill knew without any doubt at all that he was ashamed of his treatment of her, and ashamed too of offering so slender an excuse for it.

'You provoked me,' she reminded him. 'I threw it on impulse.'

Adam made no comment; his eyes were running over her figure, seeing the alluring curves and shadowed places through the diaphanous material of her nightgown. Bending, he lifted her without the slightest effort, one hand deliberately low and possessive, the other beneath her shoulders. She relaxed into a kind of sensual torpor, scarcely conscious of the smouldering embers that were soon to set her whole mind and body on fire with the longing for fulfilment. She let her head fall onto his shoulder as, with rhythmic strides, he carried her to the bed. In a few moments he was beside her, conquering the halfhearted resistance she was putting up, proving as always that he was her master, that his will was law.

The following morning Adam went off again, but Jill did not go out immediately. She was in a mood of brooding indecision, feeling one moment that she would be justified in leaving her husband, because he had flouted her wishes entirely by breaking the agreement which he himself had originally outlined, yet the next moment the pale sweet face of his mother would rise up before her and she would resign herself to whatever treatment Adam might subject her to. And through it all she was conscious of one indisputable truth: she loved her husband, and the most painful moment in her life would be the moment when she had to leave him.

It was not often that he was as unfeeling as last night, she instantly reminded herself. In fact, there never had been a night quite like that, for normally he treated her with the greatest respect. Last night he had been angry, and even though his anger had seemed to lessen, his lovemaking had been so violent that she was convinced his anger had increased again, but for what reason, she could not possibly fathom.

As she sat there, her thoughts were interrupted by the doorbell, and she waited for Charon or Rita to answer it. The voice she heard made her freeze momentarily and her heartbeat increase. Julia. . . . Surely she knew that Adam was out.

'A visitor for you, Madam Doxaros.' Charon's expressionless voice broke into her thoughts and she automatically rose from her chair. She glanced at him, noting the wooden look on his face, and guessed instinctively that he and his wife knew that Adam had been engaged to Julia. Naturally they believed it had been broken off, since Adam would never have taken servants into his confidence. He was far too arrogant ever to let them forget that they were servants, and when he wanted one of them he clapped his hands imperiously and one or the other came running.

'A visitor?' Jill looked at him inquiringly, feigning ignorance.

'Miss Komitas,' replied Charon. 'Shall I show her in?'

'I *am* in, Charon,' Julia said with dignity and authority from the open door of the sitting room in which Jill had been sitting. 'You can go!' She spoke in Greek, but of course Jill understood, instantly resenting the girl's manner. She came forward into the room as the servant departed, closing the door quietly behind him. 'Good morning,' she said to Jill in English. 'I'm very glad I found you in. I was afraid I would arrive and find you'd gone out.'

'Good morning, Miss Komitas. What is it you want with me?' So cool and composed the tone, but Jill's nerves were all awry, because she knew instinctively that the girl would never have come here on a friendly visit. There was no reason why she should.

Julia walked over to a chair and sat down, her dark eyes never leaving Jill's face. 'You're very beautiful,' was her unexpected comment. 'Adam has a weakness for beauty.'

Jill stood there, staring, waiting for whatever was to come next, but Julia did not say anything more, and as the silence stretched, Jill just had to break it. 'Perhaps,' she said quietly, 'you had better explain why you are here. At present you have me very puzzled.'

'I'm thinking of going to Mrs. Doraxos and telling her what you and Adam have done,' began Julia threateningly, 'unless of course you are willing to "play ball," as you say in England.'

Jill's pulse raced and the colour receded from her cheeks. 'You couldn't do a thing like that!' she exclaimed, shaking her head. 'It would kill her!'

'I wish she were dead already,' returned Julia without hesitation. 'She's been in my way long enough.'

'You wish her dead?' Jill stared disbelievingly at her. 'You actually wish someone dead?'

'If she had died three months ago, Adam would not have been forced to marry you.' Julia's face had paled a little, and her hands were clenched tightly in her lap. That she was under the influence of some strong emotion was evident.

'Adam said that you were not troubled by his having to marry me—' Jill stopped, then amended, 'At least, he seemed to conclude that you were in agreement with what he was doing.'

'Adam lays down the law,' returned Julia tightly, 'and because we're Greek, he believes he has a right to do so. I'm supposed to subject myself totally to his will.'

Jill made no comment; she was recalling vividly Adam's firm assertion that his fiancée had no say in the matter of his marriage to another girl.

'You didn't mean what you said about telling Adam's mother, surely?' she said at last, and Julia immediately nodded her head.

'Yes, I meant it.' Her voice was taut, her eyes glinting. 'You're far too beautiful for Adam to resist for long—I know him, remember. He told me that there was to be nothing in this marriage, that it was to be purely of convenience to solve the problem of his mother's peace of mind. I agreed—at least, I had no alternative, but do you suppose I was happy at the idea of my man marrying another girl?' A terrible bitterness edged her voice now, and Jill felt actually sorry for her. 'I hated it,' added Julia quiveringly, 'hated Mrs. Doxaros for not liking me!'

She paused, waiting, and Jill said quietly, 'Go on, Miss Komitas. You have something else to say to me.'

'I want you to leave Adam.'

'Leave . . . ?' Jill shook her head automatically. 'Mrs. Doxaros would go into a decline immediately. She's happy . . .' Jill spread her hands in a gesture of apology before she added, 'She is fond of me, very, and happy at the thought of Adam's having me for his wife. No one could be more contented than she is. Please don't make any demands that will rob her of that contentment.' Jill's voice pleaded, and so did her eyes, but Julia was not in any way affected.

'I have given you my ultimatum,' she said inexorably. 'Either you leave or I go straight to Mrs. Doxaros and tell her what the true position is—that you and Adam are not intending to stay together.'

Jill was trembling, under no illusions that the girl was not in deadly earnest; her expression, that tight mouth and the hard dark eyes—they were proof and more that Julia really meant to carry out her threat unless she, Jill, left Adam. She said at last, 'I suppose Adam told you everything—gave you the full details?' Jill wondered what he would do were he to know that Julia had been here, putting her terms before his

wife. That he would be furiously angry went
without question, but would he go as far as to
throw Julia over? It was a question Jill could not
even begin to answer, knowing as she did how
fixed his intention was to bring about the business merger.

'Yes, he did. It was your sister he intended to
marry, and she sounded so nondescript that I
wouldn't have felt myself to be in danger . . .'
Her voice trailed off, and she cast a glance at
Jill, obviously hoping that she had missed the
point, but of course that was impossible.

'You are not in any danger from me,' she said,
endeavouring to reassure her, fighting for the
happiness of her mother-in-law. 'I don't know
why you should think that you are.'

'I've already remarked on your beauty.'

'My sister was beautiful,' inserted Jill quickly.

'But I gained the impression that it would be
impossible for Adam to become attracted by her,
whereas you . . .' She flicked a hand expressive-
ly, at the same time subjecting Jill to an intense
examination as her eyes wandered from her hair
to her face and down to the dainty ankles above
smartly shod feet. 'You have everything, and the
moment I set eyes on you I was troubled. You're
just the kind of woman Adam would choose for a
pillow friend. In fact,' she added with a vicious
gritting of her teeth, 'it's a wonder he hasn't
made approaches before now. Adam's a very
passionate man.'

How Jill managed to remain totally calm and
unmoved, she would never to able to say. It

seemed that in her anxiety over her mother-in-law she was given some added quality that helped her to retain her composure in the face of what Julia had said.

'Did Adam tell you the terms under which I agreed to the marriage?' asked Jill after a pause.

'Oh, yes, I know of the financial arrangement between you.'

'If I were to leave Adam, I'd lose the money.' It no longer was of any importance to Jill, so much had happened since the terms were laid down. Loving her husband as she did, she could never even think of the reward, which, in the beginning, had been not the main incentive but certainly an important one. It was the monetary gain, plus her pity for Mrs. Doxaros, that had encouraged her to accept Adam's offer.

'I've thought of that,' returned the Greek girl blandly. 'I can give you the money—more than Adam offered, in fact.'

'You know how much he offered?' Jill looked curiously at her, and Julia said no, she had no idea how much Adam had offered.

'But I trust you to tell me,' she went on immediately. 'I feel you wouldn't lie.' A small pause, and then: 'I'd double it if you'd agree to leave.'

'I can't.'

'Is that your last word?'

'You must be reasonable,' pleaded Jill quiveringly. 'As I've said, you have nothing to fear from me. Adam won't ever change his mind about marrying you, simply because he wants the merger with your father's firm.'

'I'm not so sure, now that I've seen you. . . .' Again Julia's voice trailed away into silence. But she resumed after a pause, 'Adam's not capable of falling in love, but he's certainly the kind of man to desire, physically, a girl like you—No, please do not interrupt! I've seen the girls he's had; they were all beautiful—'

'Surely you are aware of your own beauty,' Jill had to say, thinking that this was the strangest and most improbable conversation that could ever have occurred. 'If *I* appeal to Adam, then I am very sure *you* do, too.' The words came slowly, reluctantly, for it was difficult to admit, loving Adam as she did, that another girl would appeal to him just as much as she herself did. It seemed that he had been a rake, and Jill rather thought he always would be. He had already intimated that, after he and Julia were married, he and she would have their lovers. She said, speaking her thoughts aloud, 'It strikes me as very strange that you are so philosophical regarding your marriage to Adam. Don't you want to be in love with your husband?'

For a moment there was silence, and as she noticed the Greek girl's changing expression, Jill knew what answer she would hear.

'I love Adam. And now you know why I want you to leave. If you stay and he . . . he becomes intimate with you, then he'll not let you go until he tires of you—even if his mother dies in the meantime. I shall be waiting for years, maybe.'

'You believe that he would tire of me?'

'I know he would.' Confidently, she added at once, 'He tires of every woman he has.'

'And yet you want to marry him?'

'I love him,' she repeated.

'But he doesn't know?'

The Greek girl shook her head. 'He believes it is merely a business arrangement, an ordinary arranged marriage of the kind that is customary in our country.'

'And the merger is, in effect, your dowry?' Jill was frowning heavily at the idea of Adam being quite so mercenary as to have offered for Julia sololy to obtain the dowry she could give him.

'My father wants to retire; he is a very old man. He is very pleased with the arrangement he made with Adam, and if it wasn't for his mother, we'd have been married by now.'

'She knew that the merger would have been effected if you and Adam had married?'

'Yes, she knew, but Mrs. Doxaros does not believe in the dowry system, and added to that, she has always disliked me. She told Adam she would die unhappy if he married me; she would also die unhappy if he didn't marry at all.' Julia stopped a moment, her mouth tight, her dark eyes glittering like an animal's. 'She is a selfish old woman, and I hate her!'

Jill made no comment on this, for although she knew that Mrs. Doxaros was a dear, sweet woman, she could at the same time fully understand Julia's attitude toward her.

'To get back to this matter of my leaving

Adam,' said Jill after a small pause, 'you must know that I wouldn't break my promise to him?'

A harsh expression covered Julia's face. 'It is that or I go straight to Mrs. Doxaros and tell her just how she has been deceived. I shall tell her that you did it for money. What would she think about you then?' added Julia with a sneer of contempt. 'And what would she think of her son, to do a thing like that?'

'She would know he'd done it for her sake,' Jill pointed out reasonably, but said no more, simply because Mrs. Doxaros would scarcely find comfort in the knowledge that Adam had done it for her, because she would know at the same time that Adam's intention had been to marry Julia once she was dead. It would be more than enough to make her have a heart attack, thought Jill, desperately unhappy.

'She would never forgive him, all the same,' stated Julia emphatically, and Jill could not argue that point, because she held the same belief herself.

'If you do this,' she said at length, 'you'll probably lose Adam altogether, because *he* will never forgive *you.*'

Julia seemed not to be affected by that. 'Adam's set his heart on the merger. He's a tough businessman—but you must realise that, for otherwise he would never have become engaged to me.'

So philosophically did Julia treat the matter, thought Jill, wondering how long it would be before the absurd custom of arranged marriages was wiped out in the countries of the East.

Greece was very Eastern, having been ruled by the Turks for so long. Things were changing now, and had been for some time, but as Adam had once said, custom dies hard. He had also said that in the large towns, and where the more wealthy and educated classes were concerned, the custom of arranged marriages and dowries was rapidly dying out. She supposed, viewing it objectively, that the arrangement Adam had made with Julia's father could not be classed, categorically, as an arranged marriage with a dowry in the offing. Many people married for the purpose of increasing their assets—even in England this took place, especially among the aristocracy.

'I am in deadly earnest.' Julia's voice cut into the silence, her voice vibrant with meaning but her expression now controlled. She was dignified, coolly composed in every way, but very determined. She spoke forcefully, going on to remind Jill that she had no intention of delaying the matter. 'You have to make up your mind immediately,' she added finally, and again a deep silence enshrouded the high-ceilinged, elegant sitting room.

At last Jill said, a plea in her voice, 'You must give me some time, Miss Komitas. I can't possibly make up my mind without thinking very seriously about it.'

At first it seemed that the Greek girl would remain adamant, but after a thoughtful moment she nodded her head and said yes, she would give Jill twenty-four hours in which to make her decision.

'Here's my card,' she offered, having taken it from her handbag. 'Telephone me no later than eleven o'clock tomorrow morning.' A short, significant pause before she added in soft but threatening tones, 'If I do not get the call, I shall see Mrs. Doxaros and tell her everything.'

'You know where she is at present?'

'Adam told me last evening when he was walking with me to my table in the restaurant. She is in Athens, but you will soon be returning to Corina. I shall go there to see her.' Julia paused a moment. 'If you tell Adam that I have been here, and that I have put my terms before you, then no matter what your decision, I shall see his mother. So it will not be in her interests for you to mention this visit to your . . . to Adam.'

Jill looked at her, fully aware of her inability to mention the word 'husband,' and once again she could understand her feelings. 'You need not have worried,' she returned coldly. 'I had no intention of telling Adam you had been here.' She had already pondered the matter and decided that to do so would only make matters worse, because, knowing what her husband's temper was like, she had no illusions as to what state of mind he would be in. And in the end the situation would only be the same: Julia's ultimatum would still stand.

'I'll phone you, whatever my decision,' promised Jill, a terrible feeling of despair enveloping her because she could see no other escape than acceptance of the girl's ultimatum, which meant leaving Adam almost immediately—

leaving him forever, never to see him again. Only now did she fully realise that she had been subconsciously clinging to a tiny thread of hope that by some miracle her husband would fall in love with her. Yes, somewhere in the far recesses of her mind, optimism had remained alive, even though, consciously, she was resigned to the parting when Adam's mother died.

'Please do.' Julia rose, the dignity of a queen in her movements. Looking at her, so tall and slim and beautiful, Jill was forced to own that she and Adam would make a most strikingly handsome couple and, to all outward appearances, would be admirably suited. 'I shall arrange for you to be paid—' A wave of Jill's hand stopped her on the instant, and she stared at her across the room, a frown on her face. 'I promised to pay you, to compensate . . .' Her voice trailed off, coming to a halt again as she saw Jill's expression.

'I don't want your money,' Jill told her shortly. 'Do you really suppose I would sink to accepting a bribe from you?'

'It wouldn't be a bribe. You made a bargain with Adam—'

'But not with you. Please do not mention it again.' Anger bit deeply into Jill's voice, and her brown eyes glinted. 'I shall make my decision, let you have it, and as far as you and I are concerned, that will be the end of it.'

'You're angry?'

'I'm indignant at the idea of your offering me money!' She moved to the door and opened it. 'Good morning, Miss Komitas.'

'You are very arrogant,' observed the Greek girl coldly. 'I don't understand why Mrs. Doxaros should like you better than me.' Her voice suddenly had a break in it, and Jill frowned involuntarily, again feeling a little rush of pity for the girl, for in a way she was in the same position as Jill herself—in love with a man who did not love her.

'I'm sorry,' she found herself saying, but her face was unsmiling, and she let the girl go without another word, relieved to close the door behind her.

It was very difficult to be natural with Adam when he arrived at the flat at five-thirty that afternoon. He had tried to get back earlier, so as to spend the afternoon with her, but had phoned to say it was impossible. Jill was glad; it gave her more time for considering her problem and making her decision. If she left, then undoubtedly Mrs. Doxaros would be heartbroken; if she stayed, her faith in her son and daughter-in-law would be shattered. After a nightmare period of mind-searching, of making decisions and then almost immediately breaking them, Jill felt drained and mentally weakened by the time Adam arrived, but she did somehow manage to appear happy. At any rate, he obviously did not notice anything, because he asked no questions of her, except, of course, about what she had been doing with her day.

'Looking around the city,' she lied. 'Athens is a place to linger and poke about and explore. I never ever get tired of it.'

His gaze was strange, unfathomable. 'There's no doubt that you are really taken with the city.'

She nodded. 'Yes, Adam. I certainly am. It was a wonderful experience. I was lucky.'

'You talk as if it were all in the past.' Again that strange look in his eyes, that unreadable expression.

Jill said nothing, but she was thinking that it very soon would be in the past, for her decision was made: she would leave, choosing what she believed was the lesser of two evils. At least Mrs. Doxaros would have nothing against her son. That she would be thoroughly disillusioned with her daughter-in-law was excruciatingly painful to Jill, but there was no alternative. She had her plan made already: she would go from the flat tomorrow, while Adam was out, leaving a note to say that she wanted to be with Gilbert and so she was going back on her word. That was all, until the divorce. She marvelled at the calm way in which the decision had come to her, only moments ago, and now as she chatted to Adam while they sat over a cup of tea brought to them on the balcony by Charon, she was in a state of mental lethargy in which nothing mattered anymore, and nothing hurt. It was a sort of sensation akin to delayed shock, she thought, fully prepared for the reaction which must inevitably follow later. But for the present her manner was natural, and when later they were ready to go in the car to pick up his mother, she was strangely insensible to anything but the prospect of the drive, and the actual meeting with her mother-in-law could not be visualised, no matter how hard she tried.

It was just as they were about to leave the flat that the phone rang. Adam answered it, returning to the sitting room with the information that his mother had been persuaded to stay another night.

'Is she all right?' asked Jill anxiously.

'Yes, she's fine. She just wanted to have another night with them, and all day tomorrow. We leave the following morning for home.'

The following morning she would not be here. . . .

'So I won't see your mother tonight, then?' Only as the question was being voiced did Jill realise how absurd it was. Adam was staring at her in some puzzlement, and she went slightly red. 'Of course I won't,' she murmured, feeling exceedingly foolish. But that was nothing compared to the weight of misery she carried within her. To have everything ended already was something she had never quite foreseen, not so soon. At one time she had wished her mother-in-law would live for many years yet, just so that she and Adam could be together. Well, Mrs. Doxaros might live for years, but she, Jill, would not be here.

Tears were tight and painful behind her eyes, but she contrived to prevent them from falling. She heard her husband say, 'I think we'll dine out this evening, then. I'll tell Rita not to continue with the meal she's preparing.'

They dined at a *taverna* in the Plaka, the oldest quarter of modern Athens, nestling be-

neath the ramparts of the Acropolis, its narrow
streets and lanes lined with quaint single- or
double-storied houses, many of which had small
gardens or courtyards, but almost all of which
had been turned into *tavernas*, nightclubs or
bars. *Bouzouki* music drifted out from almost
every one of them to entertain the passersby,
both local and foreign. High above the carnival
of nightlife rose the sacred temples of the Acropolis, magnificent against the dark dome of a
Grecian sky. By common consent they later
made their way to the point through which, if
one were familiar with the area, access to the
ancient site could be made without entering
through the turnstile. It was a region of gardens
and rough ground, with wild vegetation growing
on the hard, rain-thirsty land. As they wandered
through it, the clouds parted to let the brilliant
ball of the moon through, its light positive,
intense, and to Jill, caught in a web of magic as
she invariably was in this incredible city—and
much more so now that she had Adam with
her—the light was deeply disturbing; she was
physically sensible to its mystic glow upon the
sacred precincts, highlighting their beauty,
seeming to dissolve all the centuries between.
She was suddenly living in the Golden Age of
Athens, when, every fourth year, there was held
the great Panathenaic Procession, when, in a
magnificent model ship, there would be carried
the goddess Athena's new robe, which would be
borne aloft in the mighty procession as the
ship's sail. *Kores* would carry offerings of flowers to the goddess, and athletes the olive branch-

es they had won in the Panathenaic Games.
Then these maidens and men would stand aside
while shepherds led in garlanded animals to be
offered as sacrifices to Athena, whose forty-
foot-high statue, fashioned by Phidias in gold
and ivory, stood in the stately Parthenon, the
most famous and beautiful building in the whole
of the Western world.

'Where are your thoughts, Jill?'

Adam's voice recalled her to the present, but
for a moment she did not answer him, because
she was half-wishing he had not disturbed her
fanciful visions, her return to the city's glorious
past. But eventually she said, 'I was dreaming,
Adam, of the past, and imagining I was there at
the Panathenaic Procession, watching it all.
What a glorious history your country has!'

'Pagan history?'

'Oh, I have read much more than the mythology,' she returned, with a promptness that made
him smile.

'You love this city—most certainly you do.'
There was something arresting in his voice, and
his footsteps were slowing down.

'Yes,' she quivered, 'I do love it. I'm sure there
is no city in the world to compare with it for
beauty and the fascination of its past.'

He paused a moment, thoughtfully. 'It all
depends on your particular likes and dislikes.
There are many beautiful cities in the world,
Jill. You have not travelled much, remember.'

'I shall love Athens best, no matter how much
I travel.'

Adam made no comment on that; and in any case he had stopped and his arms were spanning her waist, his dark eyes fixed on her upturned face. She forced a smile to eyes that were ready to cry, for she was carrying the heavy weight of utter despair in her heart. Little did he know that she was treasuring every moment of this interlude with him, storing up memories to help her through the lonely years ahead, for she now knew not only that she would never marry Gilbert, but that she would never marry *any* other man. Adam had all the love in her heart, and so she had little to give to anyone else.

He bent his head, taking her softly parted lips beneath his own, his manner carrying all the familiar male arrogance and mastery she knew so well, and yet, somehow, he seemed almost tender with her as his hands caressed her lovely body, his fingers moving slowly as if he would prolong the exploration, savouring every delightful moment. She quivered against him, her arms curling around his neck. If only this night could go on forever, she thought, the terrible weight of misery coiled completely round her heart. But tomorrow would be another day ... and a new life beginning for her. . . .

Jill broke a window in order to get into the villa, then she went straight out and bought a new lock, which she had no difficulty in attaching herself. Although the villa had been well taken care of, Jill found it bleak and depressing the moment she entered it, and it

seemed impossible that she had been so thrilled
with it when she bought it and started to furnish
it, partly with things she had shipped over from
England, and partly with things she bought in
Athens. It seemed dark and bleak and unfriend-
ly, yet she knew that the impression was only
the result of the way she was feeling—lost and
lonely and desperately unhappy. What would
Adam think of her, breaking her word like that?
He had broken his word, too, but, strangely, that
appeared of minor importance compared to
what she had done. If only she could have
explained, given him a reason other than the
one she had, which was not only untrue but also
weak in the extreme. She had tried to find some
better way of wording her letter to him, but in
the end had given up, feeling that it could not
matter anyway. She and Adam would never
meet again, so it did not really matter what he
thought of her. Theirs had been a business deal,
a contract which she had broken. That his
mother would suffer was certain, and Jill
shirked the added misery of thinking about it,
determinedly putting it from her mind. Now and
then, though, it filtered into her thoughts, and
she would sit down and weep because it was all
wrong that, after being made so happy, Mrs.
Doxaros should then have that happiness taken
from her so soon.

Inevitably, Gilbert entered her thoughts, and
she decided to phone the *cafeneion* where they
had first met. The proprietor would convey a
message to him, asking him to phone her here,

at the villa. She would then be frank with him
and say that she wanted to put an end to their
affair. But after she tried several times to get
through and failed, she eventually gave up,
deciding to try again the following day, which
she did, with the same result. Wondering if the
telephone-directory people had given her the
wrong number, she phoned them again and
received the information that the telephone at
the café had recently been removed. So that was
that. Gilbert would never know what had happened, simply because she did not have his
address and, therefore, was unable to write to
him.

A week went by, and then another two days,
with Jill's misery increasing all the time. She
felt that if only she had all her possessions with
her she would feel better, but she could hardly
tell Adam where to send them. To add to her
misery was her state of indecision, for she could
not make up her mind what to do. Much as she
adored Athens, she felt that she could not stay
either here or anywhere else in Greece. Yet if she
returned to England, she would have to begin all
over again, looking for a place to live—and she
knew that, inflation being what it was, she
would have to settle for a flat rather than a
house. She detested flats and having to tolerate
other people's noise and often unwanted neigh-
bourliness. In a house she would have complete
privacy, as she had here, in her little villa. She
went out to see an estate agent, asking how
much it would fetch; it was too small for a

family, he said, and had no need to add that
most Greeks had large families.

'There are very few other people who want
such a small place,' he added finally, and was so
indifferent that Jill left his office immediately,
resigned to getting very little for the villa if she
did decide to sell it. She bought all the newspa-
pers, scanning the appropriate columns, seeking a job, but there was nothing, and she even
went back to the travel agency to see if they
were in need of an assistant, but they had no
vacancies.

What must she do? There seemed to be no
substance in her thoughts or ideas; she was like
a ship without a rudder, floundering in strange
waters, fearful of the future. She thought of her
sister and the possibility of asking to be tempo-
rarily accommodated in the flat she shared with
her friend. But this was soon rejected, for Susie
would be bound to jeer and say it served Jill
right for marrying Adam.

At last Jill went out to the shops to get herself
something to eat; it was a physical diversion, but
not a mental one, as she had hoped, for she
carried her problems with her, and when at last
she was coming back and was in sight of the
pretty little villa, with its bougainvillaea and
poinsettia, its flaring hibiscus bush, and the
exotic flowers she had planted when she took
possession of the house, she was actually crying,
the hot tears rolling unchecked down her
cheeks. Several cars were, as usual, parked
along the road, their owners having gone into

the *taverna* for a drink or a snack of kebabs or other Greek food. It was the sight of one particular car that held her attention, for although it was not the same make as the one used in her abduction, it somehow reminded her of that terrifying experience, and automatically her pace slowed, and she proceeded very cautiously, wondering if she would see someone sitting in the car. But there was no one, and she didn't really know why she should have been so apprehensive, since history wasn't likely to repeat itself. As she drew closer to the car, she saw the name of a hire company in the rear window and concluded that a tourist had parked the car there.

She opened the gate and went in, closing it behind her. The narrow path to the villa required weeding, she thought; and decided to do it after she had had a bit of lunch. On reaching the front door, she suddenly froze, nerves prickling, icy fingers running along her spine.

Someone had been in the house, for the door was not quite closed. A burglar! ... And he might still be inside. Turning, she dropped the shopping bag and started to run back along the path.

'Jill!' The imperious, accented voice halted her with the efficiency of a lasso looped around her body.

'Adam ...' She scarcely heard herself utter the name, yet she added, in the same whispered tone, 'What ... what is ... is he d-doing here?' He was on the step, too tall for the roof of the tiny porch, too overpowering for the house itself. Jill, her legs nerveless and weak, her heart pounding against her ribs, was quite unable to move, and she just stood there, every vestige of colour leaving her face. Would he murder her? she thought, trying vainly to drag her eyes from the dark fury of his face. It was rigidly set, but his mouth was twisted, and Jill felt she would never witness such pagan wrath again in the whole of her life.

But even when he advanced purposefully toward her, she was unable to move. Instead, she started to cry, so overwrought were her nerves. 'Why have you . . . have you come?' she faltered as he drew closer to her. 'If it's—'

'I've come to take my wife home.' He thumbed toward the open door. 'Inside,' he ordered rough-ly. 'What the devil do you mean by trying to run away again?'

'I th-thought you were a . . . burglar,' she quavered, lifting a trembling hand to wipe the tears from her cheeks. 'How did you get in?'

'You left the back door unlocked.' He paused, staring at her. 'I was standing by the window. I thought you'd seen me.'

Feebly she shook her head. 'No,' was all she managed as she walked beside him along the path, her nerves really playing her up now, and no sooner had she entered the house and the door closed behind her than she put her face in her hands and wept bitterly into them. But they were pulled away and held within the warm strength of his, and when at length she was sufficiently composed to look up, a little gasp of disbelief escaped her at the miraculous change in his expression. 'Adam,' she faltered, her body feeling drained and numbed by the relief that swept over her, for she had been sure he would do her a physical injury. 'Adam,' she whispered again, 'aren't you angry with me?' To her surprise, he made no answer, and she said, repeating the question she had already asked, 'Why have you come?'

'I've just told you, to take my wife home.'

'You can't—you don't understand,' she cried frantically. 'Your mother—she's ill because of me, but—'

'Mother,' he broke in softly, 'is dead and buried.' The words came slowly, and the last remnants of his anger were erased by pain, his lips actually moving convulsively, out of control, as was the rapid pulsation of a nerve in his throat.

Jill's eyes dilated. 'Dead. . . .' She pulled her hands from his, then had to hold onto a chair for support. 'Oh, no, I killed her, and yet what could I do—?'

'Mother never knew you'd left me,' broke in her husband gently. 'She had a heart attack and died instantly, at the home of her friends.'

'She never knew . . . ?' Relief battled with several other emotions, and then suddenly her brain refused to function because she was over-taxing it with too many questions at once. But she did eventually manage to say, her tones husky with emotion and regret, 'I'm so sorry,

Adam. She was such a wonderful person, and I'm grateful that she liked me.' Her eyes were lifted to his, glistening with tears, all else forgotten except the sad fact that Mrs. Doxaros was dead.

'It was for the best, under the circumstances,' he returned, and now a harsh note had entered his voice. 'Had she lived, and known you had left me . . .' He broke off, frowning, as if impatient with himself for mentioning that which no longer mattered. 'Jill, why didn't you come to me, dear, instead of running away like that?'

'I couldn't—you don't understand. . . .' Her voice trailed off to a bewildered silence because it had suddenly occurred to her that there was something here that *she* did not understand. 'You j-just called me . . . "dear. . . ."' She stopped, feeling foolish.

Faintly, he smiled, and reached for her hand. 'I love you, darling; that's the first and most important thing I have to say— No, dearest, please don't interrupt, even though a dozen questions are on your tongue. Let me go on, and you'll soon understand everything.' For a silent moment he held her close to his heart, but then he led her to the sofa and they sat close together while he talked. Listening as carefully as her chaotic thoughts would allow, Jill learned that Adam had scarcely finished reading her note when the phone rang and he was told that his mother was dead. She had collapsed and died within a few seconds, suffering no pain at all. Adam then said that if he had known Jill was at

the villa he would certainly have come to re-
trieve her immediately, before anything, but as
she had mentioned Gilbert in her note, his
natural conclusion was that she had taken a
ferry back to Corina. His mother had asked to be
buried on the island, and while he dealt with the
problems of transportation and the funeral, he
also had men out looking for Jill, but none of
them could find her. Then, almost immediately
after the funeral, Gilbert had arrived at the villa
asking for Jill.

'You can imagine my astonishment,' Adam
went on, looking at his wife now as if he would
like to give her a sound shaking. 'It was obvious
that you weren't on the island, that Gilbert had
nothing to do with your going away and that the
note you left me was a lie to cover up something
else altogether. I sent Gilbert off with the information that you were my wife and would stay
my wife.'

He stopped for a moment, giving Jill the
chance to speak, but all she said was, 'Please go
on, Adam. What did you do then?'

'I phoned Charon to ask if anything unusual
had happened on the morning of your departure,
and he said no, but he did mention that you'd
had a visitor the previous day.' Adam stopped,
and Jill shivered at the change in his expression.
'I came to Athens, arriving very late last night,
and saw Julia this morning.' His voice had
sharpened, his eyes taken on a metallic glint. 'I
very soon got it all out of her,' he gritted
savagely. 'I could have killed her! She'd already

had a hint from me that I was no longer sure about the merger—'

'She had?' Jill looked interrogatingly at him. 'She never mentioned anything like that.'

'She wouldn't, naturally, because she still hoped it would go through eventually.'

'You told her the engagement was off?'

'*She* broke it off—said she knew she had done wrong and that I'd never forgive her if I found out. She saw it was hopeless at that point anyway. She knew what I barely knew myself, that I love you.'

'I feel sorry for her,' murmured Jill, but she could not let herself dwell for long on Julia, who, with a dowry like that, would soon find a husband. Besides, Adam was speaking again, saying that he had known for some time that Jill was affecting him more than any other woman he had ever known.

'I was falling in love with you, obviously,' he went on, and now his voice was edged with a tender quality that made Jill forget everything except the fact that he cared, that he was hers for always. 'I had felt for some time that you were beginning to feel something for me, too, and on the yacht I came very near to telling you of my feelings. Then you shattered me by saying you'd rather be with Gilbert—'

'I lied,' she broke in regretfully, 'but of course you know that now. You see, darling, I was afraid you might guess at my feelings for you, and as I never thought you'd ever return my love, I had to do something to help my pride, and so when you asked if I'd rather be with Gilbert, I said yes.' She looked at him through a mist of tears, and he kissed her then and dried her eyes.

'It was all my fault right from the start,' he offered freely. 'I was unwilling to admit to what seemed at that time to be a weakness. I had been set on the merger for a long time; I was engaged to Julia, and you don't need me to tell you just how binding a betrothal is in Greece. There seemed so much against my falling in love with you that I was determined to fight it. After all,' he added with a wry smile, 'I've had affectionate feelings for women before, many times, but this . . .' He broke off, shaking his head. 'It was too strong for me, dearest. I really don't know why I didn't realise it sooner.' He paused in thought. 'I knew it for certain that evening when we came from the wedding and had the meal at the *taverna* on the beach.'

'I remember that evening so well,' she murmured reflectively, then went on to mention the impression she had had earlier, when they were strolling along the lanes in the village. 'I had a strange feeling that you were fighting something that was difficult to fight,' she ended, and sent him a sidelong glance and saw him nod his head.

'I was fighting my love for you at that time, too,' he confessed with a wry expression on his handsome face. 'So when you asked if anything was wrong, I snapped at you, didn't I?' Jill let that pass, because it was no longer of the slightest importance to her. 'But it was becom-

ing too strong for me,' he admitted wryly again.
'Yet I managed to maintain an attitude of indifference, if you remember?' Again Jill let his
words pass, and Adam added with a smile, 'But
when the heart dictates, the head doesn't really
stand much chance, does it?'

Jill was silent a moment, digesting all he had
told her. 'How could you have been so very sure
I'd want to come back to you?' she asked curiously at length, and again her husband smiled,
this time a little crookedly and most attractively.

'A man usually knows if his wife's in love with
him or not. And I finally saw what I should have
seen before, that you *did* love me, and that I had
made you afraid to say so.'

'But I wasn't supposed to fall in love with you,'
she broke in, without quite knowing why.

'Shall we leave any arguments for a later
date?' he suggested. 'For the present, love, all I
want to do is kiss you and hold you close to my
heart.' And suiting the action to the words, he
held her quivering body to him, enfolding it
lovingly with hands that were infinitely gentle.
His eyes on her face were filled with tender
emotion, and Jill, her arms sliding into his coat
to encircle his waist, lifted her face willingly, all
the love and adoration she felt for him shining in
her eyes.

'Is it true?' she was asking a long while later,
when, flushed and dishevelled, she was being
held at arm's length, her husband's dark face
registering faint amusement at her appearance.

'It's true, my beloved,' he answered in tones

vibrant with meaning. 'I adore you and I always will.'

Jill tried to speak, but as emotion blocked her throat, she merely nestled close in her husband's arms, finding a resting place for her head against his wildly beating heart.

15-Day Free Trial Offer
6 Silhouette Romances

6 Silhouette Romances, free for 15 days! We'll send you 6 new Silhouette Romances to keep for 15 days, absolutely free! If you decide not to keep them, send them back to us. We'll pay the return postage. You pay nothing.

Free Home Delivery. But if you enjoy them as much as we think you will, keep them by paying us the retail price of just $1.50 each. We'll pay all shipping and handling charges. You'll then automatically become a member of the Silhouette Book Club, and will receive 6 more new Silhouette Romances every month and a bill for $9.00. That's the same price you'd pay in the store, but you get the convenience of home delivery.

Read every book we publish. The Silhouette Book Club is the way to make sure you'll be able to receive every new romance we publish.

This offer expires July 31, 1981

Silhouette Book Club, Dept. SBA17B
120 Brighton Road, Clifton, NJ 07012

Please send me 6 Silhouette Romances to keep for 15 days, absolutely free. I understand I am not obligated to join the Silhouette Book Club unless I decide to keep them.

NAME_____

ADDRESS_____

CITY_____ STATE_____ ZIP_____

Silhouette Romance

ROMANCE THE WAY IT USED TO BE...
AND COULD BE AGAIN

Contemporary romances for today's women.
Each month, six very special love stories will be yours
from SILHOUETTE. Look for them wherever books are sold
or order now from the coupon below.

$1.50 each

SILHOUETTE BOOKS, Department SB/1
1230 Avenue of the Americas, New York, N.Y. 10020

Please send me the books I have checked above. I am enclosing $_____
(please add 50¢ to cover postage and handling for each order, N.Y.S. and N.Y.C.
residents please add appropriate sales tax). Send check or money order—no
cash or C.O.D.s please. Allow up to six weeks for delivery.

NAME _____

ADDRESS _____

CITY _____ STATE/ZIP _____

READERS' COMMENTS ON SILHOUETTE ROMANCES:

"Every one was written with the utmost care. The story of each captures one's interest early in the plot and holds it all through until the end."

—P.B.,* Summersville, West Virginia

"Silhouette Books are so refreshing that they take you into different worlds. . . . They bring love, happiness and romance into my life. I hope Silhouette goes on forever."

—B.K., Mauldin, South Carolina

"What I really enjoy about your books is they happen in different parts of the U.S.A. and various parts of the world. . . ."—P.M., Tulia, Texas

"I was happy to see another romance-type book available on the market—Silhouette—and look forward to reading them all."

—E.N., Washington, D.C.

"The Silhouette Romances are done exceptionally well. They are so descriptive . . ."

—F.A., Golden, Colorado

* names available on request